BLACK LOTUS 2

LOTUS 2

THE VOW

BY K'WAN

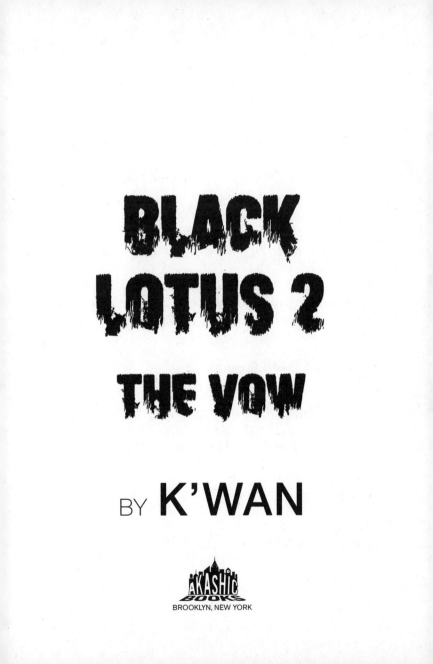

AKASHIC
BOOKS

BROOKLYN, NEW YORK

Published by Akashic Books
©2020 K'wan

Hardcover ISBN-13: 978-1-61775-778-5
Paperback ISBN-13: 978-1-61775-767-9
Library of Congress Control Number: 2019935262

Akashic Books
Brooklyn, New York
Twitter: @AkashicBooks
Facebook: AkashicBooks
E-mail: info@akashicbooks.com
Website: www.akashicbooks.com

Dedicated to the pieces of me that I lost
between the creation and publication of this story.

Denise S. Joseph
11/28/78–9/2/19

William "Jamal" Greene
3/25/54–6/9/20

PROLOGUE

Run! The word exploded in Francis's head. And run he did. He darted across the street and into an alley between two brownstones, one of which was under construction. It was dark and hard to see; he tripped over a loose cinder block, and would have landed on his face had his hands not broken the fall. His pistol escaped his grip and slid across the concrete, lying there exposed. He wasn't worried about anyone seeing it and calling the police. In fact, he'd have welcomed a visit from New York's finest at that moment. He cast a nervous glance over his shoulder before collecting his weapon and continuing.

Francis hopped a short fence at the end of the yard and landed in a vacant lot. Old tires and other oddities sat within the long-neglected grass and weeds. Francis started to slow down, but a large rottweiler, barreling toward him, changed his mind. He thought about just shooting the dog but reasoned that he might need whatever bullets he had left. He'd lost count blocks ago. Running top speed, he hit the fence on the opposite side and bounded over it. The rottweiler snapped at him, but only came away with the cuff of his jeans.

Francis found himself near the Laundromat on 131st and Fifth Avenue. The block held a sprinkling of people, mostly crackheads at that time of night, but they were witness. Francis looked back through the alley and saw that he was no longer being followed. Even if his pursuer were still on his trail, the dog would be a nice surprise. Tucking his gun, he made quick steps up the dark block.

When Francis felt like he had a large enough lead, he spared a moment to catch his breath. He ran his hand across his molasses-black forehead and it came away drenched with sweat. There was a time he could've run a mile without so much as getting winded, but that was before the cigarettes and booze. The thought of a smoke sent his hand fishing for a Newport in his pocket. He lit the cancer stick and exhaled a cloud, wondering where it all went wrong.

That morning had started out like any other. Francis got up, dressed, gargled with two nips of cheap whiskey, and went to work. He clocked in at his nine-to-five and then slid off to his *other* job. Not long after, he got a call to meet with his "associate" about the end result of the task he'd been assigned. He had expected as much, considering what had gone down. In truth, he had planned on reaching out himself if the associate hadn't beaten him to it. He would hear the man out and then decide whether he was going to break his jaw or one of his arms. Somebody had fucked up.

Francis was what you would call a hustler. He had a decent-paying gig, but from time to time he still did things he wasn't supposed to on the side for extra money, like this job with his associate. The one that was currently burning his life to the ground and trying to take him with it.

The associate was a man with whom Francis had done frequent business. He knew who to go to for dirty work. They had made quite a few dollars together over the last couple of months, and this one promised to be the sweetest score of them all. It would be quick and more than worth the trouble. The catch was that it had to go down immediately. They had a small window, and once it closed there wouldn't be another one.

The associate's tips had always been good up to that point, but Francis was still hesitant. He didn't generally do jobs without vetting them, but the weight of what he owed to bookies and back alimony was riding him. This pushed Francis to go against his better judgment and take the job. That's when everything went bad. Francis had made a desperate move, and it would cost him. How much was yet to be determined.

Shortly after his meeting with the associate, Francis called his job and notified them that he would be taking an emergency leave of absence. His superiors weren't happy because it was such short notice, but Francis had the vacation time, so there was nothing they could do. He shot home, packed a few essentials, and planned to get in the wind. He tossed his bag into the trunk of his 2003 Altima and slid behind the wheel. He was going to hit I-95; outside of gas and piss breaks he had no intention of stopping until he crossed the Georgia state line. Until things cooled off in New York, he'd crash with a friend in the Georgia police.

He was just about to put the car in gear when an odd sensation washed over him. It was the feeling you got when someone was watching you. He scanned both sides of the street and didn't see anyone, except a woman pushing a stroller and a cluster of boys huddled in front of the corner store. Francis shrugged off the feeling and pulled out into the evening traffic.

The Altima pushed up Seventh Avenue, doing about sixty. He was worried about quite a few things, but getting pulled over wasn't one of them. Any blue-and-white cruiser that made the mistake of stopping him would quickly realize that they had wasted their time. Francis was connected.

He fished a Newport from his pack and pushed in

the car's cigarette lighter. While waiting for it to heat up, he contemplated making a pit stop in Maryland. He had a lady friend who lived out that way who could do some magical things with her mouth. A good blow job and a hot meal might be exactly what he needed to take the edge off his nerves. As he was pressing the end of the lighter to his cigarette, his eyes drifted up to his rearview and saw something that made him swerve. He wasn't alone. There was a shadowy figure in the backseat.

"What the fuck?" Francis gasped.

"Not *what*, Francis. *Who*," the shadow corrected him. "The angel of death has come to pay a visit on you this evening."

Francis caught the glint of something shiny as they passed under a streetlight—a blade. "Sorry, I'm not really up for company tonight." He jerked the wheel to the right just as the shadow attacked. The car lurched to one side, knocking the intruder off-balance. Instead of slicing Francis's throat as intended, the blade cut into his shoulder. Francis felt his arm go numb and lost control of the vehicle. Before he could right its course, the Altima slammed into the back of a parked car.

When his head hit the steering wheel, Francis must've blacked out, because the next thing he knew he was being pulled from the car. Though disoriented, his survival instincts were still fully intact. He yanked his Glock from his shoulder holster and shoved it at whoever was grabbing him. He was about to pull the trigger, thinking it was the shadow, but instead found himself staring up at a startled white man. "What are you doing?" Francis wasn't sure if he was asking the white man or himself.

"You . . . you were in an accident," the Good Samaritan stammered. "I was trying to help."

"Back the fuck up!" Francis ordered. Blood was running down the side of his face and dripping onto the ground. He tried to stand but felt the world around him swim. He must have hit his head harder than he thought.

"That's a nasty wound you got. Lay still and I'll call an ambulance." The Good Samaritan whipped out a cell phone and started punching numbers. Francis was about to tell him that it was unnecessary, but he didn't have to. The man suddenly froze, eyes wide in shock as if he had just seen something horrifying. He gargled something, before blood started running down his chin and he pitched forward onto the ground next to Francis. Standing over them was the shadow.

For the first time Francis was able to get a good look at his attacker. He was slender yet built, wearing a black bodysuit and armor. There were two pistols strapped to his thighs and a harness crisscrossing his chest, holding more blades. A black mask covered his face, with something Francis couldn't quite make out marked on the forehead. If death were to ever assume a physical form, there was no doubt in Francis's mind that he was staring at it.

"Francis Cobb," the shadow began in his mechanical voice, "I have come to pass sentence on you for the crimes you have committed. Are you prepared to be judged?"

"Judge *this!*" Francis tried to bring his gun into play. As he brought it up, the shadow's hand closed around the barrel and applied pressure. Francis watched in disbelief as it bent, rendering it useless. "What are you?"

"I am the strong right arm of God . . . the Maiden Sword of Justice. I am the antidote for the sickness infecting this world."

"What's going on out here?" The owner of the store the Altima had crashed in front of came out to investigate. For a moment the shadow was distracted, and that was all the time Francis needed to make his escape.

Francis took off down the street, trying to run yet only managing a speedy hobble. He was in a world of pain, but had to fight through it if he planned on surviving. He spared a glance over his shoulder to see if the killer was still after him, and he was. The assassin wasn't running. It was more like he would disappear into one patch of shadow and reappear in another, closing the distance between them. It would only be a matter of time before Francis was caught, unless a miracle happened—and it did. A cube truck was turning the corner just ahead. The truck almost clipped Francis as he limped across its path. It cut the killer off from his trail just long enough for Francis to disappear down a dark alley. He had been running ever since.

Francis knew that he had escaped by sheer luck. If it weren't for him knowing the area better than his pursuer, and that big-ass dog in the yard, he'd probably be stiff as a log. He knew not to press his luck further. Most of his belongings were still in the trunk of his car, though he had a little cash on him. Hopefully it was enough to get him on the next thing smoking out of town.

His cigarette singeing his fingers let him know that it was done, so he flicked it away. No sooner had the butt hit the ground than Francis heard something whistle past his ear, followed by a prick of pain. He thought a mosquito had bitten him, but when he touched his fingers to his lobe, they came away bloody. A few feet away he noticed a silver dart sticking out of the tire of a car. He'd been found!

Francis's eyes shot to the doorway behind him. At first there was only darkness, but then something spilled from it—the shadow. How could he have caught up so quickly? There was no time to ponder it. Francis had to get away. He turned to run, but didn't get very far as the shadow let loose another dart. This one cut through the tendon on the back of his leg and dropped him. The shadow took his time stalking Francis as he tried to crawl away.

"Death is the only thing in life that is truly inevitable," the shadow said. Francis rolled over and tried to raise his gun to get off another shot, but the shadow kicked it away. "It doesn't matter how far we run or how well we think we've hidden ourselves. When it's our time, it's just our time."

The shadow was nearly on top of Francis. In the light Francis was able to get a better look. The mask covering his enemy's face was of a dull black that reflected no light; the marking on the forehead wasn't a marking at all, but a carving. When the shadow straddled Francis's chest, he was able to make it out: it was a black flower.

"Do you know who the fuck I am?" Francis tried to sound as if he wasn't scared to death. He figured, just maybe, if the shadow realized who he worked for, he may think twice about committing a capital offense.

"Of course I do. The mongoose has been dispatched to kill the snake."

Francis's blood ran cold. If he wasn't sure before, those words left no question as to what this was about.

The shadow deftly slid two of the daggers from his harness and twirled them expertly between his fingers, then straddled Francis's chest. He pressed his knees into his shoulders, keeping his arms spread out. It was then that Francis noticed an odd smell. Mingled under the musty leather of his bodysuit was something sweet. It was jasmine. Not the fragrance but the plant. Francis was familiar with the scent because jasmine had been his mother's favorite.

"A vow is the most sacred of oaths, and you have broken yours. Repent and I'll make your death a swift one," the shadow promised.

"What vow?" Francis was genuinely confused.

"The one you took the day you graduated from the academy. Instead of serving and protecting, you've lied and corrupted. For this you must be judged." The shadow drove the daggers through Francis's outstretched palms, crucifying him to the ground.

"Jesus!" Francis howled.

"He died for our sins as you shall die for yours." The shadow slipped a pistol from his right thigh and braced the barrel underneath Francis's chin. "You were blinded by greed and have lost your way, but I will set you back on the path. The innocent blood spilled will be the life-giving nectar that waters your grave."

"That wasn't on me," Francis managed to croak. "I

was just hired to do a job. I didn't kill anybody! Why should I have to die?"

The shadow pondered the question momentarily. "Because it was written."

PART I

IT WAS WRITTEN

CHAPTER 1

Thirteen hours prior

Kahllah sat at her desk, reading over her story for the fifth time. She had been working on it for weeks to make sure it read cleanly when it was published in *Real Talk*.

Real Talk was her dream, a magazine geared toward urban and working-class people. It was fast becoming one of the hottest magazines on the stands, but it had originally been little more than a blog started by two college girls, Kahllah and her best friend Audrey. The blog had gotten so big around campus that the two girls, years later, decided to test it in print. With Kahllah's savings, they ran off five thousand copies and took their show on the road, pitching to every independent retailer they could reach in Kahllah's beat-up Honda. Just a couple years after their first road trip, the magazine was now carried by over one hundred retailers in several states, and boasted an impressive online readership. Not bad for two orphans.

When the letters on her computer screen started

dancing around, Kahllah knew it was time to take a break. She stood up and stretched her five-nine frame, trying to relieve the stiffness in her back. She flinched as she felt the tenderness in her shoulder. Instinctively her hand went to the spot, fingers tracing the raised scar beneath her shirt. Had the bullet struck her three inches higher, it would've likely taken her head off. The shooting had happened six months ago, but the incident remained fresh in her mind.

She ran her fingers through her jet-black hair and rubbed her scalp, feeling the resistance of tangles. It had been awhile since she treated herself to more than a wash and set. Kahllah rarely bothered with primping. Unlike Audrey, who refused to leave the house without at least a light face beat, Kahllah was simple. A little lip gloss and a ponytail and she was ready to tackle the world.

Kahllah possessed a natural beauty—bronzed skin and an angelic face. Her eyes always danced between butterscotch brown and a dull hazel. Guessing her ethnicity was nearly impossible. Some mistook her for an Arab, others saw a touch of Caribbean in her. She'd been born in a small Middle Eastern village that sat on the edge of a city so ravaged by war that she doubted it still existed. Not that she cared either way. Her native land held nothing for her but the horrible memories of what she once was.

While most American children were fortunate enough to have childhoods, even those born to less than favorable conditions, Kahllah had no idea what it was like to be a kid. She lost her mother at six and her father at nine. Before her eleventh birthday, she was the property of slavers and placed on loan to whoever had enough coin to purchase a night with her. When she thought life couldn't get any worse, she was sold to a wealthy Nigerian man. He was as rich as he was evil, and subjected Kahllah to atrocities far worse than anything she had endured previously. Those were dark years. Often she prayed for death to take her away. Then came the night when God finally answered; the Nigerian was murdered.

Kahllah slid her desk drawer open, in search of her planner. She had quite a few things to do today, including lunch with Audrey. She found the leather-bound booklet under a stack of mail that she had yet to open. They were mostly bills that she'd get around to later. But she noticed something else tucked into the drawer: a copy of the *Village Voice*. She was sure it hadn't been there when she left last night, which meant someone had come in. It appeared locking her office door each night wasn't enough.

Her first instinct was to toss the weekly newspaper and be done with it. She already knew what would be inside—the same thing that had been inside the last two that had turned up. One in her locker at the gym where she worked out, the other in the bathroom of the shop where she enjoyed her morning coffee. She wasn't sure if it was out of curiosity or habit that she flipped through the pages. Her finger surfed the classifieds, skipping through the white noise. She was looking for something in particular.

It didn't take long to find it. The headline had been carefully placed among the advertisements of people seeking companionship. "Must Love Flowers." To the casual reader it was no different from the other queries from desperate souls looking for discreet encounters. Kahllah knew better. The headline was a coded message. Someone was trying to contract the Black Lotus.

A soft knock at her door startled Kahllah. She shoved the newspaper under a stack of folders and straightened. She hoped it wasn't their editor, Mrs. Jones, pestering her about the story again. She had a lot of love for the woman, but she could be a pain in the ass. Mrs. Jones was incredibly old-fashioned in her thinking, but had a very keen eye, which was why they hired her. Before coming to work at *Real Talk*, she had spent twenty years as an English professor at Rutgers University.

"Come in," Kahllah said, a little annoyed. The door creaked open, and Kahllah relaxed her defenses when it was Woody who walked in.

Woody was one of the young neighborhood men she provided with work. When she and Audrey had first met him, he was an around-the-way knucklehead who lived in one of the neighboring buildings. You could usually find Woody posted on the corner, trying to rap to girls and hustling twenty-dollar bags of weed. He'd attempted to push up on Audrey once, but she hadn't given him the time of day. This was fortunate for Woody; his flesh was too tender for her fangs. He was a nice enough young man, but he couldn't seem to keep out of trouble. Kahllah had gotten wind that his probation officer was planning to hit him with a violation if he didn't land some sort of steady employment, so she stepped in and offered him a job. It didn't pay much, but it kept him from getting sent back to jail, so he was grateful.

"'Sup, baby girl?" Woody greeted as he strode into Kahllah's office. He rubbed his hands down over his fade, trying to look sexy. He was young, broke, and thin as a rail, but you couldn't tell him he wasn't God's gift to women.

"I'm kind of busy, Woody. What do you need?"

"It ain't about what *I* need. It's about what *you* need."

"Woody, I can't think of anything I might need from you."

"C'mon, baby. Stop acting like that, smelling all good and shit." He sniffed the air around her. "What kind of perfume is that?"

"Jasmine," she answered, the same as she had at least five times since he'd started working there. Kahllah had never been into perfume, but jasmine was a favorite scent of hers. Something about it brought her peace. She made it herself from the plants she grew in her green-house. Botany was something she'd studied since she was a little girl, and she had a working knowledge of hundreds of species of plants and their properties. Extracting different fragrances and selling them to tourists as perfume was how she'd fed herself in her early years of bondage.

"Well, it smells like a snack to me." Woody licked his lips.

"Woody, your young ass needs to quit. It ain't gonna happen."

"Why you be trying to play me? You act like you're crazy old. You only got me by like five years, if that. The important thing is that we're both grown, right?"

"Woody," she said, bumping him off the desk, "just because you smell grown, doesn't mean that you are. Now, what do you want?"

"Okay, I can take a hint. I was about to go to lunch and I wanted to know if you needed anything."

"I'm fine, thanks. But could you run this to Edna for me?" She popped a flash drive from her computer and handed it to him. "I need it proofed and uploaded to our site ASAP."

"New story?"

"Yeah. It's the interview I did with Jerome Yates."

"Ain't that the cat that killed all those people?"

"*Allegedly*," she corrected. "He's still fighting the case."

Everyone knew the story of Jerome Yates. He was arrested in connection with a shooting at a basketball tournament that left five people dead and at least a half dozen injured. The details of what went down were sketchy, but the police claimed to have his prints on the gun and a witness who placed him at the scene. To this day he proclaimed his innocence, but nobody would listen, except for Kahllah. She knew the real shooter was already dead, yet the problem she faced was proving Jerome's innocence without incriminating herself.

"He did it," Woody said matter-of-factly. "You can tell by looking at that crazy muthafucka."

"Woody, you can't judge people based on appearances."

"Bullshit, Kahllah. When the police found him, he was living in his mother's basement, collecting snuff porn. That shit screams serial killer to me."

"So, those are the facts your argument is based on?"

"Damn right!"

"Woody, if I recall correctly, you still live with your mother. And I'd be willing to bet a month's salary that you own a porno or three."

"Man, I don't need no funky movies or books, I gets mine. A real player knows what to do with a woman."

"Is that right?" She moved closer to Woody. "So, what would you do with me?" Her breath brushed across Woody's neck.

"I . . . I'd make you cum like you never did."

She stroked his cheek gently and smiled. "Woody, baby, if you go outside like that, the police might arrest you."

He glanced down and noticed the bulge in his pants, then turned his eyes away in embarrassment. "You ain't right, Kahllah!"

"And neither are you. Now go and do what I asked." She laughed as he slunk from her office.

Kahllah waited until Woody had gone before retrieving the copy of the *Village Voice* from beneath the folders. She gave it one last hard look before tossing it in the trash. Whoever the client was could find somebody else to do their dirty work. Her days of dealing in blood money were over.

CHAPTER 2

Tony Thompson sat in the passenger seat of the unmarked white van, staring idly out the window. It was just shy of ten a.m. and the sun had begun to creep higher into the sky. It shone with a brightness Tony wasn't used to as he usually didn't make it outside until after dark, unless he was out of weed. He was a member of New York City's growing number of unemployed. Had been for nearly six months. It wasn't that Tony wasn't willing to work, it was just hard finding an employer that would overlook the fact that he had done time. It didn't matter that he'd graduated high school and even managed to snag himself an associate's degree; most jobs that would hire him either wanted to hand him a mop or a spatula. Just when Tony was ready to give up and go back to slinging crack, someone came along who was willing to take a chance on him.

"You ain't falling sleep already, are ya?" Hank's gruff voice broke Tony out of his daydream. He was an older man, with sharp eyes and a square jaw largely covered by his salt-and-pepper beard.

"Nah, man. I ain't asleep. I'm just enjoying the view," Tony told him.

"I'm glad you got your eyes on your surroundings. Just make sure you don't lose focus. We're being paid to get this to where it needs to be, not watch the damn grass grow. The eagle don't land and we don't get paid." Hank eased the van into the left lane to pass a slowly moving Honda.

"And what are we transporting again?" Tony asked.

"What are you, the police?"

"You know better than that. Shit, I just want to know what's so important that we gotta roll heavy to guard it." Tony nodded toward the revolver wedged between the driver's seat and center console.

"This ain't heavy." Hank plucked the gun and held it up. "Heavy is you and five angry niggas who ain't seen a woman in months, crawling through the desert with HKs looking to whack a couple of sand rats. This ain't heavy, it's a deterrent." He put the gun back.

"You think we'll run into trouble?" Tony wasn't afraid, he just wanted to be prepared.

"Doubt it. You'd have to be a special kind of stupid to try and rob the fellas we're hauling for. Now, if you're scared, I can drop you off on the next corner and finish the run on my own."

"Man, quit trying to play me. You know my pedigree. If some shit goes down, I'll probably get to that gun before your old ass!"

Hank yanked the wheel, cutting across several lanes of traffic. Tony gasped as the older man almost caused an accident getting to the shoulder. Hank pulled the car to an abrupt stop and threw it in park. There was a serious edge to his voice: "Listen, young buck. In the event that something pops off, you just keep your fucking cool and follow my lead. I done survived two tours and an eight-year prison bid, so I don't plan on dying behind some pissy little nigga trying to play hero. We go from points A to B, get our bread, and go home to our families. That's the job. You get me?"

"Yeah, man. I get you."

For the next few minutes they rode in silence, save for an old-school CD that Hank had going in the player. From the sour set of Hank's face, Tony could tell that he was still feeling in a way about his questions, but all Tony was trying to do was figure out the score. The cats they were working for were giving them five grand apiece to deliver whatever was in the back of this van. This told Tony that it was most likely drugs. If they were getting it to the point where they could afford to pay the drivers five grand, there was no telling what kind of money they'd spend on a smart young dude who knew the ins and outs of the game, like Tony. Hank might be content as their driver, but Tony had bigger plans.

His dreams of surpassing the man who had given him a job were interrupted when a green van pulled up alongside them, from the right. The driver was wearing what looked like a rubber snake mask. Before Tony could even process what he was looking at, the side door of the green van slid open. A second man peered over at Tony. He, too, was wearing a mask; it looked like a bearded old man wearing a frumpy pointed wizard's hat, like the sorting hat from *Harry Potter* that chose which houses of Hogwarts the children would be separated into. The wizard waved his hands and, as if by magic, produced a thin metal wand with blinking lights. He made an overly dramatic sweeping gesture before jabbing the wand into Hank's van. That was when everything went to the left.

There was a popping sound, followed by a surge of energy that washed over the vehicle. The stereo died first, filling with static then falling silent. Next was the on-board computer system. Every light on the dashboard lit up like Christmas, before winking out. Tony held on for dear life as the engine died and the steering wheel began to seize up, causing the van to fishtail as Hank struggled for control. It went off the road and slammed into a metal guardrail. Tony lurched forward, smashing his face on the dashboard; without his seat belt he'd likely have gone through the windshield. Though the van stopped, Tony's world was spinning. His nose throbbed, likely broken, and blood dripped down his face and stained his shirt. He looked out the broken windshield and saw that the green van had parked in front of them. Several people wearing masks spilled out and approached. It was clear what was going down—they were being robbed.

Tony made to reach for the revolver, but Hank stopped him. "Two tours and a bid," the older man whispered.

There were four of them, three men and a woman. All wore dark coveralls and different animal masks. The snake-headed driver was the first to approach. He was carrying a gun like nothing Tony had ever seen— nearly three feet long, chrome with blinking lights along the barrel that resembled the lights on the wizard's wand. It evoked the sci-fi movies Tony had loved so much as a kid. Snake ambled up the driver's side and pointed the weapon.

"Little pigs, little pigs, let us in," he sang, tapping the barrel on the window.

"Just be cool," Hank said, holding his hands above his head.

Tony heard his door being ripped open. He was confronted by a brute of a man with wide shoulders and a large head, crowned by a helmet made to resemble an elephant. Jutting from the sides were two curved iron tusks, sharpened to fine points. "Out!" he barked, grabbing Tony by the jacket and yanking him from the van. Tony skinned his hands and knees when he fell onto the gravel road.

"No need to be so rough about it, he's only the help," scolded a feminine voice. Tony looked up and found the woman standing over him. She wore a fox mask with furry red ears. "C'mon, suga. Ain't nobody gonna hurt you, so long as you play nice." Her voice, sweet, had a thick Southern accent. Fox extended a hand that was covered in an iron gauntlet.

Tony must've hesitated too long, because Mastodon grabbed him and yanked him to his feet. He shoved Tony around to the other side of the van where Snake was holding Hank at gunpoint. With him was Wizard and his pulsing wand. He and Snake seemed to be in the middle of a heated exchange. After a few ticks, Snake, in a huff, entered Hank's van. He snatched the keys from the ignition and headed around to the cargo section. A few seconds later he was back.

"None of these work," Snake announced. "Where are the keys to the back, old-timer?"

"We ain't got 'em. We only get the keys to the ignition. The cargo ain't our business," Hank explained. "I suggest you just take the whole van and figure the rest out later."

"And have you call this in as soon as we're gone?"

Mastodon barked. "The fuck? Do we look stupid to you?" Tony snickered nervously. "Oh, you think this is a joke, huh?"

"Pay the boy no mind. He's slow," Hank said.

"Did I ask you to play defense attorney?" With the top of his helmet, Mastodon rammed Hank's chest. He barely put anything behind it, but the force knocked the wind out of Hank and sent him flying. "Next time, you get the tusks!"

Hank lay on the ground feeling like he'd been hit by a truck. He could barely catch his breath and his ears were ringing. His eyes, fortunately, were working just fine, but what he saw caused all the color to drain from his face. Mastodon and Fox were exchanging words while Wizard appeared to mediate, and Snake still looked unsure of what to do next—but it wasn't any of the bandits who had Hank's attention, it was Tony. He was inching toward the open van door, and there was no question in Hank's mind as to what he intended to do and how it would turn out. That was the moment a well-laid plan had gone totally to shit.

Tony dove through the open van door and went for the gun. Hank could see Tony positioning himself, taking aim. He probably would've blown Snake's head clean off, had Mastodon not intervened. At the same time Tony pulled the trigger, the brute slammed his helmet into the door with so much force that it nearly cut Tony in half. He was done, but Mastodon wasn't. He hit a button on the side of his helmet and the tusks extended like spears, puncturing the door and the young man within. The tusks made a wet noise when Mastodon pulled them free and dropped Tony's lifeless body to the ground.

"We were gonna give the shit up. You didn't have to do that. He was only a stupid kid!" Hank bellowed.

"And now he's a stain." Mastodon laughed, tusks still slick with Tony's blood.

"We said no bodies," Snake snapped. "That was the deal!" His earlier bravado was gone.

"And who the fuck is you to tell me anything?" Mastodon snarled. "I'm about sick of you bumping your gums like you call the shots!"

"If you're sick, I got something that'll make you feel better." Snake tightened his grip on his weapon.

"You two assholes done?" Wizard said. "This ain't recess, we still on the clock. Fox, pop this can open so we can get gone."

Fox made her way to the back of the van, followed by the others. A thick lock secured the cargo doors. Fox flexed her fingers and metallic claws sprang from the tips of her gauntlets. Two quick slashes and the lock fell away in pieces.

"I got this." Snake bumped Fox aside before she could open the doors. This was his score . . . something he had brought to the table, and he felt that gave him the right to be the first to lay eyes on the prize. When he popped the doors the first thing he noticed was the smell. It was like something rotting in the heat.

"Wait, is that . . ." Fox began, before covering her mouth and turning her eyes away in disgust. There was no cocaine in the van, only trouble.

"I think the word you're looking for is *shit*," Hank said. "And you all just stepped into a steaming pile of it. There's some important people that ain't gonna take too kindly to what you all have done."

"Us??" Snake roared. "We didn't have shit to do with that!"

"True enough, but I think you're gonna have a hard time convincing the old man of that." Hank gave a smug grin. "As we speak there's a little bird somewhere singing a song with all your names in the lyrics."

Wizard stood before Hank and glared down at him. The pieces were now falling into place. He drew a gun, a black revolver, and placed it to Hank's head. "You set this whole thing up, didn't you?"

"Sorry, son. That's above my pay grade. My job was to dangle the carrot, not spring the trap."

"What the fuck does that mean?" Fox asked.

"It means we've been double-crossed." Wizard looked at Snake.

"Wait a minute," said Snake. "I didn't have anything to do with this. I'm just as shocked as the rest of you." It was true. This job was supposed to be a defining moment for him within the ranks of the crew.

"We'll see," Wizard said. "What's the game here, old man?"

"Ain't no game, youngster. Let me give you some cold truth: the minute you opened that van, it started the shot clock on what's left of your lives. I'll see you boys in hell."

"Tell the devil to hold a place for us!" Mastodon, in an incredible show of strength, lifted Hank off his feet with one hand. Using one of his tusks, he gored the driver, spilling his intestines onto the ground, then tossed him aside as if he were trash.

"Fuck you do that for, man?" Snake rasped. "We should've made him talk and tried to figure out what's going on!"

"Ain't nothing to figure," Wizard said, staring into the back of the van.

"This is bad. If he thinks we had anything to do with this—"

"He won't," Wizard assured Fox. "Bleach all this shit, then burn the van. We were never here."

CHAPTER 3

Kahllah had some time before she needed to meet Audrey at Amy Ruth's, so she decided to walk. *Real Talk* was located on 125th, so it wouldn't take her very long to get there. Besides, it was a beautiful day and the exercise would do her good.

Kahllah loved strolling through Harlem. She had long been fascinated by the sights and sounds of the historic place. It was nothing like Brooklyn, where she'd first landed upon moving to the United States.

Shortly after her savior had smuggled her into America, he found himself in a bit of legal trouble. As he hadn't yet had a chance to put the girl's affairs in order, Kahllah found herself a ward of the state for a time and was placed in a group home while everything was sorted out. The home was unisex, with the boys on the top two floors and the girls on the bottom. Piling in as many children as they could, no matter how awkward the situation, was just one more way for the city to cut costs. There were quite a few kids carrying on sexual relationships. Most were doing so willingly, but some were not. Kahllah opted for neither.

It wasn't like they hadn't tried her. Kahllah had always been a pretty girl. At a young age she showed early signs of womanhood. The mistake people had always made with her was thinking that, because she was pretty, she couldn't fight. They were very wrong. Her harsh upbringing had yielded natural survival instincts. When they came at her singularly, she fought them off with her fists. When they came in groups, she showed her skills with a knife. She didn't always win the confrontations, but she never stopped fighting.

Kahllah passed the book vendors on 125th Street and peeked to see what new titles had come out. She didn't really read urban novels, but a book called *Street Dreams* had caught her attention awhile back, opening her up to the whole movement. She didn't read them as faithfully as Audrey did, but when an urban novel caught her attention, she'd support the author.

After purchasing a book, Kahllah continued toward Lenox Avenue. When she rounded the corner, a group of white kids came pouring out of the train station. They were all dressed in hip-hop gear and swearing loudly. She was sure she even heard one of them say *nigga*. Kahllah hated hearing people of color use the word, but it especially irritated her when someone of noncolor tossed it around. A part of her wanted to stop the young white boy and educate him, but that would likely lead to him saying something slick, which would result in her kicking his ass and ruining her outfit. As tempting as it was, she let the remark slide and continued on her way.

Kahllah sauntered down Lenox, taking in the sights. A few years prior, Harlem had been a mess of dope fiends and dilapidated buildings. The dope fiends were still there, but many of the buildings weren't. Those husks of the past were now replaced by high-rise apartments filled with tenants who looked nothing like the natives, and renovated brownstones selling for three times what they'd cost ten years ago. Harlem was definitely changing.

The walk to 116th Street didn't take her long at all, and she had barely broken a sweat. Audrey probably would've complained about her aches and pains the whole way there, but never Kahllah. Her savior had raised her to believe that her body was sacred, something to treat like a temple. She ran five miles per day, watched what she ate, and worked out like a boxer training for a prizefight. She was the picture of perfect physical health, but her mental health was a different story.

There was a decent-sized crowd when she arrived at Amy Ruth's. It was one of the few spots left in Harlem that still served actual soul food and not free-range chicken with collard greens out of a can. She was almost immediately greeted by an overly chipper hostess with a bad haircut and too many teeth in her mouth.

"Hi, just to let you know, it'll be about a twenty-minute wait," the hostess said.

"I'm actually meeting someone." Kahllah began scanning the restaurant for Audrey. She wasn't hard to spot—she was sitting at a table near the rear, waving her arms like she was on fire.

As she made her way to Audrey, Kahllah happened to catch sight of a familiar face seated off to her right. He was wearing a pale-green suit, at least one size too big, and a pair of scuffed brown shoes. The outfit was a far cry from the tailored silks and Italian leathers that had once been his garments of choice. His full head of perfect black hair had begun to go gray and was thinning on top. Kahllah may not have recognized him had it not been for the scar along his jaw; it had required surgery after she broke it.

Several years earlier, Sullivan "Sully" Roth had been a prominent director-producer. His name had been attached to several critically acclaimed films, including one that was making a clean sweep of all the major film festivals. Sully was well on his way to becoming the darling of Hollywood, but his shining star had been dimmed when a dark secret was revealed.

As a great filmmaker, there had been no shortage of young wannabe starlets looking to hitch their wagons to his brand. Landing a role in a Sully Roth production could be career changing for someone trying to get discovered. In his last film he had made a superstar out of a young woman who had been a cashier the year before. Struggling actresses were willing to do whatever it took to get in, until they discovered exactly how high the price of admission was. They found themselves victims of Sully's sexual fetishes. Most were too embarrassed by what they'd been forced to do to come forward, and the few who did were dismissed as opportunists. This was the case with a young Latina actress named Elaine Rodriguez.

According to what Elaine had told the police, she was invited to Sully's office under the pretense of auditioning for an upcoming film, only to be pressured into performing sexual acts for the role. When she refused, Sully got rough, and she barely escaped without being raped. Of course, Sully used his influence to spin the story: he painted a picture of her as just another fame-hungry groupie trying to sleep her way to the top, and the people ate it up. Why wouldn't they? He was a rich and powerful filmmaker, while she was a poor Puerto Rican girl from the Bronx. Elaine had all but given up on receiving any kind of justice, until her story reached the Black Lotus.

Kahllah was sympathetic to the girl, so she decided to bring an end to Sully and his preying. Her initial thoughts were to kill him, but then she had a better idea. She called in some favors and managed to land a meeting with Sully, to which she arrived wearing a recording device. She told him she was an aspiring actress looking for her big break. Sully took one look at her with that long black hair and exotic features and was on her like a dog on a bone. Over drinks, he promised to make her a star while trying to get into her pants. The man touched and pawed her like an octopus; she fought the urge to vomit as his hands explored her. When she felt she had enough dirt on him, she tried to leave, faking intoxication, but Sully didn't take rejection well. Getting rough, he tried to force himself on her. This is when she broke his jaw and escaped. She could've very easily killed him, but death would've been too swift and too merciful for such a worm. She had something else in mind.

Kahllah had taken the dirt to a friend she had at the newspaper. By the next morning the recording had been leaked and Sully found himself fodder for the headlines. Other women started coming forward with their own tales of what they had suffered at the hands of the producer, and it created a shit storm of bad press. The same Hollywood power players who had once backed him now refused to touch him. As quickly as Sully's star had risen, it fell even faster. He spent a year in prison. The last anyone heard, he was making B-rate porno films out of a basement in Queens. He was ruined, and had Kahllah to thank for it.

Pulling her mind from the past, she focused on the present, her lunch date with Audrey. Audrey was a light-skinned woman of average height, with a round face and full lips. Today she was sporting her hair in large, blond goddess braids. She was thick, but wore her weight confidently.

"Is that who I think it is?" Audrey greeted her. She was looking past Kahllah at the man in the pale-green suit.

"Yes, Sully Roth."

"Man, I'd heard his life had taken a turn for the worse, but I didn't realize it had gotten *that* bad. He looks terrible!" Audrey remembered him being handsome, always well dressed. The pile of loose clothes and stress sitting at the table was neither. "I guess it's to be expected, considering you flushed his entire career down the toilet and got him thrown in prison."

Audrey had meant it as a joke, but Kahllah didn't laugh. She took no joy in the misfortune of others, even if they deserved the fate that had befallen them.

"So, did you order yet?" Kahllah changed the subject.

"No, I was waiting for you and catching up on current events. Have you seen this?" Audrey slid her iPad across the table.

It was a piece that had been published a few hours ago on the *Daily News* website. The remains of four people were discovered in a van that had been torched. Two of them had been identified as Ellie Lorton-Smith and her husband, Michael. They had just gotten married at St. Anthony's a few days prior, and had gone missing while on their way to the airport to leave for their honeymoon. Kahllah recalled seeing Ellie's uncle, Manhattan Borough President Chancellor King, on the news pleading for the safe return of his niece and her husband. But the relation between the city official and the corpses wasn't what troubled Kahllah. It was the picture of the van, which had been burned to a crisp, save for a few patches of metal. She stared at what was left of the cargo doors and saw what looked like claw marks.

"Wow," Kahllah muttered.

"Somebody killed Chancellor King's niece and her husband, and all you can think to say is *wow*? Do you know what kind of shit is about to hit the fan?"

Indeed, Kahllah did. Audrey was likely speaking about the backlash that would come from murdering the relative of a city official, but Kahllah knew the face Chancellor King wore when the cameras weren't rolling. There would be hell to pay in the streets, she was sure.

"This is the kind of newsworthy stuff we need to be covering," Audrey said. "Do you think you can reach out to some of your contacts and see if we can get an interview or at least a quote from someone in King's inner circle?"

"I doubt it," Kahllah lied. "Anyhow, I'm surprised you beat me here, considering you're generally late to everything."

"I was already in the area visiting a friend." Audrey smiled devilishly.

"You nasty little whore," Kahllah joked. "Whose man are you sleeping with now?"

"Me?"

"Come on, heifer. Spill it."

Before Audrey could respond, the waitress came over. She was a nice-looking girl, not gorgeous but cute. Her face was smallish like a pug, but her smile wide and inviting. Kahllah took her measure. It was just something she did out of habit, sizing up strangers for strengths and weaknesses. The waitress must've mistaken Kahllah's analysis for flirtation, because her smile grew even wider.

Kahllah picked up on this and shut her down: "We're ready to order now."

The waitress's smile faded and it was back to the business of service. Kahllah ordered the liver and onions, while Audrey had the barbecue chicken platter. They both requested iced tea, Kahllah wanting hers unsweetened.

When the waitress left, Kahllah went back to her pressing. "So?"

"Okay, I met this guy—"

"What else is new?"

"Do you wanna hear the story or not?"

"Sorry."

Audrey rolled her eyes. "Anyhow, I got invited to the soft opening of this place called Voodoo. Remember I tried to get you to go with me, but you flaked?"

"Yes, I remember." The name might've been new, but the venue wasn't. The place had once been called Purge. Back then it was a rest haven for thugs and miscreants. Kahllah had visited once while working her other "job." Not long after, the club shut down. Rumor had it that a dead body had been discovered in a utility closet.

"I was on the fence about going, because I didn't want to fly solo, but I decided what the hell? So I get cute and roll up only to find the place super dead. There was nothing but old heads wearing cheap cologne telling stories about all the money they *used to have.*"

"Sounds like your type of place," Kahllah teased.

"At least I *have* a type!" Audrey shot back. "After around an hour fighting off perverts, I'm about ready to get out of there when the bartender places a bottle of champagne in front of me. I'm looking at the man all kinds of crazy, because I know I didn't order it and damn well couldn't afford to pay for it. I'm ready to send it back until the bartender points out the dude who sent it over. Honey, this man was fine with a capital *F*! He was tall, dark, and dripping in designer, just my type. He gave me this smoky look then licked his lips like LL Cool J. I damn near creamed my panties." Audrey fanned herself. "His name is Ben. We spent the whole night drinking and talking, and the next thing I knew I was at his crib climbing the walls. God blessed that man below the waist! By the time he dropped me off at my apartment the next morning, I could barely walk. I think he might be the one, girl."

Again, Kahllah wanted to say. She loved Audrey, but the girl was a bit on the loose side and a hopeless romantic. She was one of those people who went looking for love instead of letting it find her. Any man who showed her some attention could possibly be *the one*. If Kahllah had a dollar for every time she helped mend Audrey's broken heart, she'd be one of the richest women in the world. "Sounds interesting."

"Interesting?" Audrey frowned. "I just told you I could've possibly met my soul mate, and that's all you can say?"

"Audrey." Kahllah leaned on her elbows. "You're my girl, and you know I love you, but you're a horrible judge of character."

"How do you figure that?"

"Let's see. There was Marcus. He was the be-all and end-all, let you tell it. That was all well and good, but you had to share him with his wife and other mistress. Then there was Lance. He was cool too, except he kept stealing from you to support his undercover coke habit. Then there was Bill. Bill was the best of the lot, because you felt you had a spiritual connection to him. Unfortunately, so did his gay lover. Is it just me, or is there a pattern here?"

When Kahllah saw Audrey dip her head in shame, she realized she may have gone too far. Kahllah could sometimes be so emotionally detached that it made her insensitive to the feelings of others. It wasn't intentional; this was born from years of mental conditioning. Emotions were for the weak and the weak were unfit.

"I'm sorry, I didn't mean it like that."

"No, you're right. I need to guard my heart a little closer," Audrey said. "I know you didn't say it to hurt me. You're just trying to look out."

Kahllah tried to lighten the mood: "So, other than make your panties wet, what does this Ben character do?"

"Ben has a very diverse portfolio." Audrey sounded proud. "He primarily plays the real estate game, flipping and investing. He owns a bunch of properties around the city. He even has a stake in Voodoo."

"Is that right?" Kahllah knew where the conversation was headed; she was just waiting for the other shoe to drop. Audrey had a bad habit of mixing her sex life with business.

"You know, everybody is trying to get the exclusive on Ben and his partner, with how fast they're coming up and all. But I got Ben to agree to give it to *Real Talk*. How would you feel about us covering the opening of Voodoo tonight?"

And there it was. The thread that bound Audrey's loins to their company. "I thought they had their grand opening. Isn't that where you met Ben?"

Audrey shook her head. "That was a *soft* opening. I'm talking about their coming-out party." Seeing the hesitation on her friend's face, Audrey pressed on. "K, Voodoo's grand opening and the men behind it have been the talk of the city for weeks. Ben says there'll be some real high-profile people there, and we'll even get to sit down with the owner, a dude they call Magic."

"The name alone tells me everything I need to know about him." She'd heard the name before but wasn't sure where. What she did know was that nicknames usually spoke volumes about their holders. This Magic was probably full of tricks.

"You of all people should know that you can't judge a book by its cover. It'll be a great networking event, and we could probably make some important connections. It'll be good for the magazine."

This had more to do with Audrey trying to get under Ben than it did with the magazine, but pointing this out would likely lead to an argument, and Kahllah wasn't in the mood. Instead she tried to exit through the back door. "I don't know, this is really short notice. I'd have to find something to wear . . . get my hair done."

"Girl, please! You got that good shit. All you gotta do is throw some water and gel in it and you're good to go."

"Very funny. And besides, you know how I feel about crowds. It's likely to trigger my anxiety. You've become a pretty damn good journalist over the last few years. Why can't you just cover the event yourself?"

"I could, but I'd make more of an impression if I walked in with you."

"Me? Why?"

"Because you're eye candy!" Audrey responded. "Those exotic features, that beautiful hair . . . even if no one knew who we were, they'd want to know after getting a look at you."

"Why do I feel like you're trying to pimp me for your own personal gains?"

"We got the personal out of the way the night I went home with Ben. This is all business, baby. Instead of pimping, see it as marketing." Audrey winked. "We both know that half the guys there will probably be sexist assholes, but they'll also be attached to major brands. Brands that we can tap into and expand our reach."

"Still sounds like flesh peddling to me."

"That's because your thinking is so damn dated. Loosen up, have a good time once in a while. Who knows, you might even find a Ben of your own. God knows you need one. You haven't been out on a date since Wolf!"

"That wasn't a date. I was conducting a follow-up interview for the story we ran on him about those two cases he worked."

"If that's what you want to call it." Audrey gave her a playful smile. "I'm still baffled about how the story started with you trying to prove he was a dirty cop and ended with you painting the portrait of an unsung hero. That Wolf must've left quite the impression on you."

"You could say that."

James Wolf, known to his NYPD comrades and the scum he hunted as Lone Wolf James, was the subject of a piece on police corruption that Kahllah had been working on awhile back. He had a reputation as a hard-nosed detective who didn't mind bending the law to the point of breaking it to get what he wanted. Plenty of rumors circulated on his dirty deeds, but no one had ever been able to catch him with his hands in the cookie jar. That was what put Kahllah on his trail. She hated dirty cops and had been determined to expose Wolf for the villain he was. At the time, Wolf was investigating what the media had dubbed the "Black Lotus killings." They were named after the rare black flowers present at each crime scene.

The latest victim had been a priest named Father Donovan Fleming. They'd found him in his church, strung up by chains like a sacrifice in some dark ritual. A respected priest being murdered in such a way caused a public outcry for justice that was heard as high as the mayor's office. When Wolf's friend and mentor Captain Marx dumped the case into his lap, it was the detective's last shot at redemption, so he took it. What nobody expected was that the Fleming murder investigation would reopen a years-old cold case, that of a little boy named Johnny Gooden who had been beaten, raped, and left to die in the snow. It was the one case Wolf had never been able to solve, and it haunted him for years. As it turned out, Father Fleming had not only been a man of the cloth, but also a serial rapist of children. Rich and powerful people had helped bury the secret, and it was Wolf who unearthed it. It ended up earning him a promotion. Although he never managed to catch the Black Lotus, it was the assassin's bread crumbs that had helped break the case and give the Goodens peace, so they were even as far as Wolf was concerned. At least until they next found themselves on opposite sides of a gun.

"I don't know, Audrey. I've got a ton of work to catch up on."

"Kahllah, we're the bosses. What are you going to do, fire yourself? If you do this for me, I'll owe you big-time."

Kahllah sighed. "Fine."

"Thanks, K! We're gonna have a blast, you watch!"

Kahllah smiled. She had agreed more out of wanting to appease Audrey than believing the event was a good idea. In fact, she was pretty sure she would regret the decision. The last time she'd entered that venue, things had gotten nasty. And one thing she'd learned from *both* her jobs was that lightning struck twice more often than it didn't.

After they finished eating, Kahllah paid the bill. As they made to leave, Audrey gave her the latest office tea from a marketing firm *Real Talk* used to work with, before they cut ties. To its credit, the firm did good work, but upper management left a lot to be desired. Its head was a notorious womanizer who would stick his dick in a brick wall if it got wet enough. He was said to have slept with nearly all of the women who worked with them.

He'd even tried his hand with Kahllah, but she shut him down. He'd been sniffing around Audrey too, and though she said nothing ever happened, Kahllah had heard a rumor to the contrary.

His latest conquest was a young and naive receptionist who had made the mistake of falling into the deep end of the pool. She hadn't been there a week before he was in her panties. The wife, Audrey narrated as they neared the exit, had paid an unexpected visit to the office and caught her husband with his fingers knuckle-deep inside the receptionist.

Kahllah was so engrossed in the tale that she accidentally collided with someone coming in as they were going out. He was handsome, in a rugged sort of way—a high forehead with wavy black hair that was just beginning to recede at the temples. The gray suit he wore fit him nearly perfectly; no doubt it had been tailored. His build was decent, bordering on athletic except for the slight bulge of his stomach. Yet his gut wasn't the only thing Kahllah noticed around his belt. A sleek black nine millimeter rested in a leather holster on his hip. His jacket did a fair enough job hiding it from the untrained eye, but Kahllah's eyes didn't miss much. Especially not concealed weapons. If she had to guess, from the cheap suit and gun model, he was a cop.

"My apologies," the man said.

"No, it was my fault," Kahllah replied. "I should've been watching where I was going."

"Nonsense, the error was on me, sweet thang. I'm normally more careful where I place my feet, but I'm afraid I was temporarily blinded by your sheer radiance."

"I've been called a lot of things in my day, but I don't think *radiant* is on the list."

"That's a shame, because it should be at the top." He smirked, showing off white teeth. "I hope I didn't hurt you."

"I'm tougher than I look."

The man was about to follow up, but he saw something in her eyes. Something that made him cautious. He nodded. "Of that I'm sure. In any event, you have my sincere apologies for my clumsiness. You ladies enjoy the rest of your day." He mock-bowed and continued inside.

"See what I mean about how men react to you?" Audrey said.

"Mm-hmm." Kahllah lingered in the doorway and watched the armed man find his way to Sully's table. Sully didn't look pleased to see him, though that didn't stop the man from taking a seat. As she studied them, she couldn't figure what a disgraced filmmaker and a cop would be rendezvousing for, in the middle of Harlem. Whatever they were up to, she doubted it was good.

"So, do you want me to come by your place and help you get ready for tonight?" Audrey asked.

Must love flowers . . . She remembered the classified ad. "No, I've got something I need to take care of first, but I'll meet you there."

CHAPTER 4

Sully Roth sat at his table in Amy Ruth's trying not to stick out, but it was harder than it sounded. Not because he was white in a soul food restaurant in the middle of Harlem. Sully was comfortable in any neighborhood, black, brown, or white. The only color he saw was green; he was about the dollar. No, what made him stand out was the fact that he was wearing a bulletproof vest one size too big, which bulged like a turtle shell under his white shirt. He was sure he looked ridiculous, but appearances be damned. His life was in danger. Sully had made a blunder of epic proportions and was now trying to do everything he could to fix things, including taking a meeting with the man who had been directly responsible for bringing the chaos down on his head in the first place. Desperate times called for desperate measures.

After nearly thirty minutes of waiting, Sully was about to give up and leave when the man finally appeared. He strode in casually as if he didn't have a care in the world, pausing for a beat to exchange words with two women on their way out. One of them, tall and dark-haired, struck him as familiar, but he couldn't see her face. He watched the exchange suspiciously, and suddenly his imagination started getting the best of him. What if the girls were part of all this? What if this was a trap and he had allowed himself to be boxed in? His eyes quickly scanned for an alternate exit but didn't find one. He was fucked!

"Why are you sitting there looking like you're trying to decide whether to shit yourself or find a bathroom?"

In plotting his escape, Sully hadn't noticed that the conversation with the girls had ended and the man he was meeting was now hovering over him.

"Ah . . . trying to remember if I locked my car door or not before I came in."

"If you're still driving that piece-of-shit Nova, I don't think you have too much to worry about. You couldn't give that bucket away, so I highly doubt anybody is going to try and steal it." The man laughed and took the seat across from Sully.

Before the conversation could continue, the waitress approached. "Can I get you something?"

"Yes, sweet thang," the man said. "I'll take a cheese-burger, rare. I like my meat tender."

"Be back in a few," she said and rushed off.

"How can you eat when the world is coming to an end, Frank?!" Sully snapped.

"Because I've been so busy cleaning up shit all morning that I haven't had a chance to grab a bite." It was meant as a joke, but Sully didn't laugh. "Why don't you relax? I think you're overreacting to this whole situation."

"Overreacting? Your guys were supposed to do a simple snatch and grab, not commit a quadruple homicide! You said your people were pros, not trigger-happy thugs!"

Frank leaned in and lowered his voice to a stern growl. "First of all, watch your tone. I'll bounce your head off of this fucking table if you ever speak to me like I'm one of those bitches who bust it open for you in your cheap movies! And second, we didn't off those kids. The driver and his boy were collateral damage, but the other two weren't on us. As I'm thinking about it, maybe it was *you* who lined all this up?"

"What?" Sully's eyes got wide. "That's ridiculous!"

"Is it? You promised that the van would be full of coke, but all we found were corpses. Maybe you've got an axe to grind with the old man and tried to use us as scapegoats."

"Wait a second, Frank. We've been doing business together for a while, and you've put quite a few dollars in my pocket. Why would I mess that up?"

"Well, somebody fucked up. I hear the old man didn't take it too well when they found his niece and her guy."

"That has got to be the understatement of the year." Sully chuckled nervously. "He was freaking livid. Word is that he's offering up a shitload of money to anybody who can make what happened to those kids right. I hear he's even reached out to the *Brotherhood*." He whispered the name, as if saying it any louder would bring on some terrible fate.

"And?"

"What do you mean *and*? Do you know what the Brotherhood is and what they specialize in?"

The Brotherhood of Blood was a secret order of assassins whose origins went back several centuries. For the right price, the Order would not only wipe out your enemies, but in some cases their families and associates as well. They were not merely contract killers, but worshippers of death.

"For the part we played in this, it ain't gonna end well unless we figure a way to get clear of it."

"You mean the part *you* played," Frank corrected. "This was your caper, so it falls on you. Me and my guys were just hired muscle."

"So, you'd really hang me out to dry?"

Frank shrugged. "Plausible deniability."

"You think you can throw a rock and hide your hand when it comes to the Brotherhood? Don't be stupid. We need each other right now. I say we head for the hills until we can figure a way out of it, or at least until it blows over."

"I ain't doing shit," Frank countered. "See, I can understand *you* being shook, but I'm not. I ain't some regular schmuck." He brandished the badge on the end of the chain beneath his shirt. "I'm the *police*, remember? Ain't nobody gonna be stupid enough to try and kill a cop."

Sully shook his head. "You just don't get it, do you? Titles and affiliations don't mean shit with the Brotherhood. There's nothing you can hide behind once they've been contracted to take you out. Not even a badge."

"You done?"

Sully realized that Frank just wasn't getting it. "Yeah, I guess I am." He dropped some cash on the table and stood. "You do what you want, but I'm about to crawl under a rock. If you were smart, you'd do the same. Good luck to you, Detective Cobb." He saluted and then made his exit.

Frank continued sitting there long after Sully had gone. He weighed the man's warning. The moment he recognized the two dead bodies in the van, he'd known that trouble was soon to follow. Though he'd pretended to be unbothered in front of Sully, Frank was no fool. His being a cop would give the average contract killer pause, but this was the Brotherhood. Would his badge protect him when the devil came to claim his due?

PART II
TAKE IT IN BLOOD

CHAPTER 5

He smelled it long before he saw it. A distinct aroma, carried on the chill evening wind and into his sensitive nose. The faintest hint of copper tickled the back of his throat and made him spit on the ground. It was a smell he could identify anywhere . . . blood. Like a hound on the trail of an elusive fox, he followed it. Even if he hadn't been texted the address forty minutes prior, he would have known where he was going. The closer he got to the source, the more pronounced the scent became.

It was there, just a few feet ahead. He could see a dark alley with beams of flashlights bouncing off the walls. A line of police tape covered the entrance, and two uniformed officers guarded the perimeter. It appeared only one was doing his job, while the other was hunched over. His hands rested on his knees, and from his mouth spilled a hot stream of bile. The color had completely drained from the man's face, giving him the appearance of a living corpse.

He neared the alley, sticking close to the shadows.

He doubted either of the uniformed officers would've noticed him even if they had been paying attention. One was focused on the meal he'd just spewed on his shoes, while the other was trying to look everywhere except the alley. They were clearly shaken. He shifted, causing the heavy gold chain hanging around his neck to rattle against his chest. It was a deliberate action to announce his presence so he wouldn't get shot by accident. Police shootings in the city were at an all-time high, and he didn't think his name would look good in headlines . . . again.

The first to notice him was the cop who had been throwing up. He watched as the pale beat walker wiped his mouth with the back of one hand and let the other rest on his service weapon. Frightened eyes said he didn't want to shoot, but trembling hands suggested he might.

"You need help with something?" the second cop said.

"I hear it's the other way around," he joked in his raspy tone.

Neither of the officers laughed. He hadn't expected them to. There was a brief moment of silence as they sized each other up. He could only imagine how he looked to these uniformed officers, dressed in a baggy gray sweat suit, white Nikes, and hair braided back into five thick cornrows. He had a slender face with heavy sideburns, ears that rose to slight points, and a deeply cleft upper lip. In certain light he almost resembled a canine. He could tell that the officers weren't quite sure what to make of him, and he didn't yet feel inclined to be forthcoming.

"Some mess you boys got in there." He glanced past them, into the alley where he could see a medical examiner taking photos of something.

"This is official police business," the cop who had been vomiting said. "You need to move along." His hand was still resting on his holstered weapon.

"If only I could." He reached inside his sweatshirt and produced a gold badge attached to a silver chain.

"Bullshit you're a cop!" the second officer scoffed.

"*True* shit. I'm Detective James Wolf."

"Wait, as in *Lone* Wolf?" the vomiter said.

"I guess my reputation precedes me." Wolf had been prepared for the skepticism and disdain he generally got from fellow officers who knew his history, and was surprised by this different reaction.

"It's an honor to meet you, sir." The officer grabbed his hand and pumped it vigorously. "You were a legend among my graduating class at the academy!"

"Thanks," Wolf said, still a bit thrown by the response.

"What the hell is a wolf?" the second officer questioned, not sold on the thug.

"Only one of the greatest detectives to ever wear a badge," his companion said. "This is the guy who solved the Gooden case."

The second officer was familiar with the case of little Johnny Gooden. It had become a headline when Wolf uncovered the fact that it had been a priest who had murdered the boy and a police captain who had buried the evidence. When the shit hit the fan, heads rolled both figuratively and literally. In solving the case, Wolf had also exposed a ring of police corruption stretching all the way down to One Police Plaza. When all was said and done, a lot of decent cops lost their jobs for looking the other way, and Wolf ended up with a promotion. While some praised him as a hero for what he had done, others branded him a traitor for turning on his own.

"So this is the cop who hunts other cops?" the second officer said. A few of the ousted cops had been his friends. He knew the detective by name, and had caught his picture in the papers, but this was his first time seeing him in the flesh.

The detective shrugged. "A wolf will hunt just about anything if it's hungry enough."

The second cop shook his head. "How could you do it, man? Bringing down your own people."

"Those weren't *my* people," Wolf shot back. "They were symptoms of the disease that's rotting this department from the inside out. I make no excuses or apologies for honoring my oath to protect and serve. I only wish that I could do it over again, so I could blow their fucking heads off instead of sticking them in cages."

"You've got a real slick mouth," the second cop.

"Trust me, my bite is far worse than my bark." Wolf drew his lips back into a sneer, flashing his long canines.

"Detective Wolf!" a female voice called from the mouth of the alley. She was tucked into the shadows, so he couldn't see much beyond her curvy silhouette, but Wolf would recognize that voice anywhere. It was time to get down to the business that had brought him here.

"You boys have a good night." Wolf shook the first cop's hand.

"See you around *real soon*." The second cop didn't veil his threat.

"I hope so. I haven't eaten pork in years, but for you, I'd gladly make an exception."

When Wolf passed the police tape, he got a better look at the woman who had called out to him. The slither of light cast into the alley from a single streetlamp kissed the gold shield resting on her ample breasts. She was five eight, with cocoa-brown skin and cropped black hair. She wore tight-fitting dark jeans that showcased her thickness—the perfect ass-to-waist ratio—and a black leather jacket that protected her from the night air. On her hip was a large silver revolver that he was pretty sure hadn't been department issued. The gun looked too big for her petite hands, but Wolf knew personally that she could not only hold the cannon, but handle it efficiently.

This was Lieutenant Tasha Grady. She and Wolf had history that stretched back to when she was just a beat walker and he was still in the missing persons division. They both came from similar backgrounds: two street kids who had clawed their way up the ranks of the NYPD. Like Wolf, Grady's career had been fast-tracked by cracking a newsworthy case sprinkled with scandal. The short version of her story was that she managed to convince the public that a man called Animal, who was rumored to have killed more people than cancer, had been secretly working with the NYPD to bring down a drug cartel. The end result was that Grady had spearheaded a bust that crippled the cocaine trade in the tristate area, and Animal received a slap on the wrist for his alleged crimes. The media ate it up, but those familiar with Animal knew that he would rather have died than work with the police. Still, the ruse went over well enough to earn Tasha Grady a promotion.

"I see you're still the social butterfly." Grady nodded toward the second cop, who was still staring daggers at Wolf.

"That ain't on me. Some of these uniforms could

stand to show a little respect when in the presence of their betters."

"Betters?" Grady looked amused. "We all bleed the same when the bullets start flying, and the only thing standing between you and the afterlife is a fellow badge. The fact that you've lost sight of that probably explains why you can't keep a partner." The minute she said this, she regretted it. "I'm sorry, you know I didn't mean that the way it sounded."

"It's all good," Wolf said as if the remark hadn't stung. Richie Dutton had been Wolf's partner and mentor in his early days of working undercover narcotics. They called him the Chameleon due to his ability to slip effortlessly in and out of criminal personas; he was so good because, at heart, he was more criminal than cop. Wolf always turned a blind eye to most of Dutton's crimes, until the day came that his mentor crossed a line he couldn't come back from. Wolf was the one who put him down. Wolf was eventually cleared of the charges—ruled a self-defense shooting—but the blood of one of his closest friends was still on his hands. It was the one stain Wolf had never been able to wash away. "So, to what do I owe the pleasure of being called out on this late night, in which we're still wearing clothes?"

"Jesus, could you at least try to show a little professionalism?" Grady glanced around to make sure no one had heard. She'd made the mistake of sleeping with Wolf once in a moment of weakness and had regretted it ever since. "A murder."

"Lieutenant, I'm sure you've got at least a half dozen competent homicide detectives working under you, so why call me all the way out here for some stiff?"

Grady lowered her eyes. "I can show you better than I can tell you."

Wolf followed the shapely lieutenant deeper into the alley. He had wondered why he only spotted two cops outside, and now he knew. The rest were crammed into the alley. Wolf had to walk sideways just to get through. Heavy police presence at a crime scene wasn't unusual, but there were at least a dozen officers, in plainclothes and uniforms. All wore dark expressions, and from some emanated a palpable anger. There was only one thing Wolf could think of that would get this sort of reaction out of a bunch of cops.

When he reached the perimeter erected by the medical examiners, his suspicions were confirmed. It was indeed one of their own laid out in the alley. The corpse was missing the top of its head and part of its face, yet Wolf was able to make the ID by the poorly done tattoo on the right forearm; it was supposed to be a snake but bore a striking resemblance to a crooked penis. He'd given the guy shit about it on more than one occasion.

They all had. The victim was none other than Detective Francis Cobb, the one cop in the department with more dirt on his name than Wolf, though Cobb had lived up to every nasty thing that was said about him. He had been suspended twice in his career for misconduct, and if the rumors were accurate, he was currently under investigation for the alleged rape of a prostitute. Without a doubt, Francis Cobb was a shitty human being, but he was still a cop, which meant there would be hell to pay over his death.

Wolf broke a long silence: "Somebody fucked ol' Frank up."

"That's putting it mildly," Grady replied. "We've got a fair idea of what happened, but I need to see it through the eyes of a wolf before giving the official word."

It wasn't the first time Wolf had been called in to assess a crime scene. He had the uncanny ability to pick up on things that sometimes went unnoticed during routine investigations.

He breached the perimeter set up by the medical examiners, careful not to disturb any of the evidence, and began his work. He closed his brain off to the white noise of the outside world—the chattering voices, squawking police radios, droning traffic—and zeroed in on the scene. The first thing he noticed was the defensive wounds on Cobb's arms and hands—he'd tried to fight his attacker off. In the palm of each hand was a hole. They could've easily been mistaken for stab wounds, yet they were too small and too clean for any knife Wolf could think of. They were the work of a stiletto, possibly some type of spike. Something else that immediately stuck out to him was the blood, or lack thereof. There was a good amount of blood pooled under Cobb's head, but no splatter, not on the walls or the floor. When someone got their head blown off, it usually left a mess.

"He didn't die here," Wolf said over his shoulder to the lieutenant. "Frank bought it somewhere else, and his body was dumped here to be discovered. Not a small dude, so it likely took a lot of effort to bring him here from wherever he was killed. The question is, why? Frank have any connection with this neighborhood?"

"Not that I know of. There isn't much out this way except a few warehouses, a cemetery, and that church, St. Anthony's."

The name hit Wolf like a jolt. St. Anthony's was the church where they had found Father Fleming's body.

"If you want," Grady said, "I can have some officers canvass the neighborhood with photos of Frank to see if it jogs anybody's memories."

"Don't waste your time or the manpower," Wolf replied. Frank's body being dumped in this particular alley in this neighborhood wasn't a random occurrence, it was a bread crumb. As he continued his examination, something nagged at him. It took a minute, but it finally came to him. "Where's his gun? You log it into evidence already?"

"No, he wasn't armed when we found him. Figured he wasn't carrying tonight."

"Guys like Frank are *always* carrying, on or off duty. Too much bad juju on them to get caught slipping. Frank been acting different lately? Change of routine in any way?"

"I heard he put in an unexpected leave of absence this afternoon."

"You should've led with that." Wolf shook his head. "I'm willing to bet that Frank was running from something. The question is, what?"

"I was hoping you could tell me," Grady said, then reached into her jacket pocket and removed a small plastic baggie. "Found it with the body. Figured it was best if this little detail didn't make it into evidence. At least not right away."

Wolf tried to keep his face neutral as he peered at the baggie. It held a small black flower. It wasn't like anything that grew in the city, but he had seen it before. "That supposed to mean something to me?"

She gave him a quizzical look. "Wolf, we've known each other too long to play games. I know how the report was written up on the Johnny Gooden case, but I also have my own theory about how you were really able to solve it and who helped." She paused. "I knew this would be personal to you, so as a courtesy I wanted to give you the first crack at making it right before I called in the big guns."

Wolf chuckled. "If you know anything about the Lotus, then you know your people won't stand a chance."

"I'm not talking about the department. After the Red Widow incident, we put certain protocols in place to ensure that our faceless friends from under the mountain would think twice about how far outside the lines they color. Protocols that I hoped I'd never have to enact— but I think a dead cop leaves me no choice."

Wolf glanced from the body back to the lieutenant. "This doesn't feel right. Regardless of whatever Cobb may have done, I can't see him attracting the attention of the Lotus."

"We both know that if the money's right, anything's possible."

"For some of them, but not all. Cobb was a bottom-feeder, and there would be no honor in killing him."

"Doesn't change the fact that a cop is dead, and the best lead we have is this calling card." She held up the baggie. "For as much as I'd like to disregard this, I can't.

Somebody has got to hang for this. The best I can do is try and delay the inevitable."

"Fuck!" Had it been anyone else, Wolf wouldn't have given a shit how it played out, but this was the Black Lotus. The time they had spent together hadn't exactly made them buddies, but there was a mutual respect. In their last encounter, they seemed to agree that there was a line in the sand; crossing it would mean war. Apparently, Wolf was the only one who had respected that line. "How much time do I have?"

"Twenty-four hours . . . maybe less," Lieutenant Grady said. "Then I gotta make it rain and turn a blind eye to whoever gets wet. You think that'll be enough time to do what needs to be done?"

Wolf shrugged. "Does it matter? By this time tomorrow, I'll have Detective Cobb's killer in shackles or I'll be dead." He took the baggie from her and headed toward the alley's exit.

"That doesn't inspire a lot of confidence!" she called after him. "Do you even know where to find the suspect?"

"Not a clue, but I know where to start looking."

CHAPTER 6

Shortly after arriving at Voodoo, Kahllah was over it. It was too crowded, too loud . . . too much of everything. Sensory overload, making her nauseous. This was why she avoided nightclubs, except for business, which was what this night was supposed to be about. So far it had been one headache after another, starting from the moment she'd agreed to come.

After having lunch with Audrey, she'd gone home to begin the task of finding something to wear, which proved to be harder than it should have been. Her wardrobe largely consisted of jeans, leggings, and body armor, none of which were appropriate for the occasion. So she had to go shopping. Shopping was probably the only thing she hated more than nightclubs. She tried on three different outfits before settling on a simple black dress and a pair of heels that had been collecting dust in the back of her closet.

After that, there was still some time before she needed to meet Audrey at Voodoo, so she decided to pop into one of the many storage units she kept around the city.

This particular one was in the Bronx. Inside sat boxes of files from jobs she had worked over the years. Most of them were coded, so she didn't have to worry about anyone stumbling across them and figuring out what her *other* job was. Ever since Audrey had shown her that article, all she'd been able to think about were the claw marks on the van. Claws that could rip metal didn't belong to any quadruped, but she knew of a two-legged beast that could inflict that kind of damage. She had been reported dead, but what if the reports were wrong? It was unlikely, but not impossible. In Kahllah's years with the Brotherhood, she had learned that nothing was impossible, including resurrection.

Time must've gotten away from her while she was strolling down memory lane, because when she checked her watch, she realized she'd been in the storage unit for over two hours. She was left with barely enough time to go home, shower, change, and get to Voodoo. Before heading to the club, however, there was a loose end she needed to tie up.

She was supposed to meet Audrey at nine p.m., but it was a quarter to ten when she finally arrived. Outside, she tried calling Audrey but got no answer, likely because she couldn't hear the phone over the blaring music. Kahllah was tempted to use this as an excuse to go home, but she didn't want to disappoint her friend.

There was a line of people trying to get in, and she reluctantly joined them.

After paying fifty bucks, Kahllah was finally admitted. The place was nicer than she remembered, but then again, the last time she was there she'd made a speedy entrance and an even speedier exit. The place had undergone a total makeover, courtesy of the new owners, and was actually quite posh with its velvet chairs and white marble floors. It was like walking into heaven.

She found Audrey seated in the VIP section, sipping champagne with a group of people wearing expensive clothes and plastic smiles. Hardly her type of crowd. Audrey waved Kahllah over and whispered something to the bouncer, who allowed Kahllah to pass through the velvet rope and sit with the beautiful people.

They had been waiting for about an hour and there was still no sign of the man who was supposed to be giving them the exclusive on Voodoo for their magazine, the elusive Magic. One thing that irritated Kahllah was people who didn't respect her time. More than once she threatened to leave, but Audrey begged her to stay put, promising that Magic would be along soon. He was handling club business, as she put it. Kahllah knew that Audrey was full of shit and stalling, but she didn't call her out on it. Instead, she busied herself people watching.

Most of the men and women gathered in their section proved to be as interesting as watching paint dry. All they talked about was what they had and who they were; they seemed substanceless, hardly worth entertaining, though the same couldn't be said about Audrey's new love interest. Ben was a handsome devil, with a smooth chocolate face and neatly trimmed salt-and-pepper goatee. He was built like a linebacker, looking to be about six four with muscles that bulged beneath his smoke-gray tailored suit. He was an imposing figure, yet handled Audrey like a gentle giant; catering to her every whim and fawning over her like a schoolboy with a crush. Audrey seemed to glow in his presence, something Kahllah hadn't seen with the other guys. It was possible that Ben's intentions with her friend were genuine, but there was something more to him than what he was showing. She knew this by the way the other guests in their section reacted to him. Nervous energy. When they laughed at his dry jokes, it was obviously from a fear of displeasing him rather than actually thinking he was funny. She even caught one guy flinch when Ben turned suddenly to reach for one of the champagne bottles. According to Audrey, Ben was a simple businessman, so what was it about him that had his entourage on edge?

You're reading too deep into this, Kahllah told herself, trying to shut off the side of her brain that was always on the hunt. She'd been retired for a while, but still had trouble letting her thoughts rest. She picked up the champagne flute that had been sitting in front of her for the better part of twenty minutes and sipped it. No sooner had it touched her tongue than a frown crossed her face. She pushed it away. It had gotten warm and flat, much like the rest of her night.

"Champagne is like revenge—best enjoyed cold," a voice whispered in her ear. Startled, Kahllah leaped to her feet and spun so abruptly that she knocked over her champagne, spilling it all over the table and her shoes. She found a man hovering over her. He was tall, not as tall as Ben, but still above average. He wore his hair in a tapered cut, with thick black waves rolling over the top. Misty green eyes, set inside a high-yellow face, drank Kahllah in. Unlike Ben, who was wearing a suit, this man wore a simple black turtleneck and black jeans. Hanging from his neck was a gold chain with a bejeweled pendant shaped like a magician's hat. Before Ben announced him, she knew who he was.

"Damn, Magic! Looks like you're losing your touch with the ladies," Ben teased.

"Sorry about that," Magic said to Kahllah. He grabbed one of the white cloth napkins from the table and went down on one knee to clean up the mess.

Kahllah watched as he dabbed the moisture from her shoes. The whole time he was looking up at her with those green eyes, like a cobra trying to hypnotize a mongoose. She broke his gaze and focused on her shoes. She noticed that, in addition to the champagne, something red came away on the cloth. "I got it." She quickly snatched the napkin from him.

A hint of a smile touched the corners of his pink mouth as he stood. "Hi, I'm—"

"Late," she cut him off. She didn't mean to come across as rude, but she was still a little rattled about him being able to sneak up on her. People getting the drop on Kahllah was something that almost never happened.

"Kahllah!" Audrey shot her a look. "Magic, this is my partner—"

"Ms. Kahllah El-Amin," he interjected. "I'm familiar. I've been a fan of your work for a very long time."

"Really? You don't strike me as the type of guy who reads *Real Talk*," Kahllah said.

"I don't, and truthfully, I'd never even heard of it until Ben brought it to my attention the other day. However, I've been keeping tabs on some of your other work. Your name is ringing in the streets."

"What's that supposed to mean?" Kahllah responded.

"The work you do in the inner cities. You're quite the hell-raiser when it comes to advocating for the rights of the underprivileged and wronged. I really dug the piece you wrote a few years ago on the Back 2 Life program."

The Back 2 Life program had been set up by two rival gang members who'd managed to put their differences aside to focus on something bigger, the future. The program's main purpose was to help young men and women looking to break away from gang culture and rejoin society. They provided résumé-building services, conflict-resolution strategies, and job-readiness classes. In the beginning, they'd been a small, privately funded organization, operating off the goodwill of the communities they were trying to service. But once Kahllah's article was published, a national spotlight fell on them and the good work they were doing.

"Oh," Kahllah said, relieved. Still unused to retirement, she was seeing phantom enemies everywhere.

Magic smiled. "Your story made it possible for the Back 2 Life program to get the help it needed to really get out there and make a difference."

"I was happy to do it. I have a lot of respect for John and C-Lo and the work they do."

"So do I. C-Lo taught me a lot about what it means to be a man." Magic rolled up a sleeve and revealed a tattoo on his forearm that read *H.G.C.* "Harlem Gangsta Crip," he said with a hint of pride. "I was one of the first kids to come through the program when they started it."

"I'd have never guessed," Kahllah said. Magic looked

more like a model than a gangbanger—but looks, of course, could be deceiving.

"Because I've worked really hard to clean up my image."

"We've come a long way since banging and pulling armed robberies, huh, Magic?" Ben chimed in.

"Indeed we have, and there is still so much further for us to go."

"From the looks of this place, I'd say you're well on your way," Kahllah said.

"Voodoo is my baby, but it's only one piece of the puzzle. I've got big plans, Kahllah. Very big plans." Magic rubbed his hands together.

"Well, that's why we're here. We want to find out more about the man behind the plan."

For the next half hour, Kahllah picked the brain of the man known as Magic. He was quite candid during their chat, sharing with her his highs and lows, hopes and dreams. His moniker came from his knack for disappearing at signs of trouble. Over the years he'd had more than a few close calls with the law and his life. One incident he touched on briefly was when he had gotten jammed up with his partner Archie during a traffic stop. The police found a gun and weed in the car. The gun belonged to Magic, and with him already being a convicted felon and on probation, he knew he was fucked. That was when Archie stepped up and claimed ownership. Archie's reasoning was that he had been a career criminal and in the streets for decades, while Magic's star had only begun to rise. Going to prison would've robbed him of the opportunity to take his shot at greatness. Besides, Archie was already on the run for a shooting that he had been involved in, so he figured it wouldn't hurt to add a few more years to the lengthy bid he'd be getting. Magic had never forgotten his friend's sacrifice, and promised that he wouldn't squander his second chance. This was when he turned his attention to creating something legitimate. By the end of their conversation, Kahllah had a newfound respect for the reformed hustler.

As they were wrapping up the interview, Ben tapped Magic's shoulder. "Six o'clock," he said, nodding at something just beyond where they were sitting.

Magic's mood seemed to darken at this. He mumbled something to Kahllah that sounded like "Be right back," but his jaw was clenched so tight she couldn't be sure. Kahllah watched as Magic picked his way through the crowd, and went to greet someone. It was an older fellow, dressed in a suit and flanked by two hard-faced men, also wearing suits. Bodyguards, no doubt. Kahllah had been staring at unfamiliar faces all night, but this one she knew very well.

CHAPTER 7

M agic traversed the logjam of people inside Voodoo to receive his unexpected guest. Ben remained in the VIP area with the women from the magazine, but Magic could feel his eyes on him, watching to see if there'd be trouble. For all their sakes, Magic hoped there wouldn't be. He took a deep breath and mustered his most convincing smile before greeting the King.

Chancellor King was a very important man. His family had operated out of the section of New York formerly known as Five Points for three generations, and he currently sat as its reigning king. They had their hands in just about everything, including drugs and prostitution. Nothing moved south of Houston Street without the King receiving his taste. Recently he had turned his attention to playing politics, currently holding the position of Manhattan borough president, leaving his oldest son, Ghost, to handle the family's less-than-savory dealings. Voodoo was a spot that a man like King tended to avoid, so his presence was unusual, especially on opening night. Magic had a good idea of why he was here; he just hoped that his face didn't betray this.

"Mr. King! What an honor it is to have you with us tonight."

Magic went to shake the man's hand, but one of the bodyguards blocked him. Magic wasn't an enemy, but he wasn't a friend either. When dealing with men like Chancellor King, it didn't really matter; you were either family or you weren't. The old man paused as if trying to decide whether to let Magic approach. After what felt like a lifetime, he waved his guards back and allowed it.

"You should've told me you were coming. I'd have had a private section prepared for you."

"I never announce my comings and goings," Chancellor said. "I like to keep people on their toes. Don't you know that by now? Besides, I'm not here for drinks, I'm here for answers. I'm sure by now you've heard what's happened?"

"Yes, my condolences to you and your family. It was a sad situation, to be sure."

"A sad situation?" Chancellor's nostrils flared. "My wife's niece and her new husband are murdered on their honeymoon, and you call that a *situation*?"

"I didn't mean any disrespect, Mr. King."

"Killed them like they were dogs! Found the bodies burned to a crisp. Had to identify them by their dental records. These bastards didn't even leave enough of them for a proper burial."

"If there's anything I can do, just say the word."

"I'm glad you feel that way." Chancellor's face took on a look that made Magic nervous. "Word on the streets is that they were killed by a crew. Not just any crew. A highly skilled group of individuals using high-tech weapons. Sound familiar?"

"With all due respect, Mr. King, you should know better. Murder was never my thing. I was a robber. Besides all that, I've been retired for a while now. I don't pull heists anymore. I'm legit."

"So it would seem." Chancellor looked around the club. "What about your old crew? They retired too?"

"Ben is my partner here, Archie is doing fifteen years of state time, and Butch got killed out in Pennsylvania last year." Magic shrugged. "Ain't nobody left."

"And your cousin, the pretty one? Wasn't he running around with you boys for a time? What was his name again?"

"A passing fascination, and he's since come to his senses." That was all Magic would say. Chancellor was asking after Magic's cousin and old running buddy, Red. The cousins had been as thick as thieves back in the day. This was around when Magic had first hooked in with the weapons suppliers who would help push his career to the next level. Red had been a college kid who got his kicks from hanging around with gangsters. Magic letting him get mixed up in his business was a recipe for disaster, but Magic didn't see it coming until Red crossed him on a score and made off with the money. Magic didn't track Red down and kill him for the same reason he wouldn't reveal his name to King: Red was his favorite aunt's only son. Magic hadn't spoken to his cousin in years, and the last he'd heard, Red had abandoned his criminal aspirations and gone back to college.

"Not everyone is smart enough to get out," Chancellor said with a smirk. "Some folks keep playing until they're taken out."

And there it was. He hadn't threatened Magic directly, but it was there, hiding beneath that sour-ass grin. Chancellor's eyes bore into Magic, as if he were a human lie detector. Just then, one of the waitresses approached Magic and whispered something into his ear.

"Mr. King," Magic said, "I hate to seem rude, but I have some club business that I need to attend to. I'd be honored if you'd stay as my personal guest. I'll have Molly take you to one of our private booths."

"Thank you, but no. Much like yourself, I have some business to attend to. My niece's killers ain't gonna catch themselves."

"I'll keep my ear to the streets, and if I hear anything, I'll be sure to let you know."

"No worries, Magic. I'm sure we'll be speaking again

sooner than later." Chancellor gave a sly smile before turning on his heels and walking off.

Magic stood there for a time, watching the old man and his bodyguards move through the crowd. It wasn't until he was out of sight that Magic released the breath he'd unconsciously been holding. Whether or not Chancellor believed him was anyone's guess. The King of Five Points had an impenetrable poker face. What Magic knew was that nothing good would come of this.

CHAPTER 8

"Everything okay?" Kahllah asked once Magic returned to their section. She could tell from his face that something was weighing on him.

"Yeah, just saying hello to an old friend."

"I didn't know Chancellor King had any friends," Kahllah half joked. She knew just who King was and what he was about.

"What he want?" Ben cut in.

"We'll talk about it later," Magic said.

"He's got some nerve, peacocking his old ass in our joint like he owns it," Ben said. "If he knows like I know, he'll take that shit back down to Five Points."

"I said we'll discuss it later!"

Ben finally caught on and let it go.

"Listen, I think we've taken up enough of your time tonight," Kahllah said. "You guys probably have things to do, so maybe it's time we call it a night?" She stood to leave, but Magic stopped her with a soft grasp of her wrist.

"Nonsense." He eased her back into her seat. "You

can't just rush off before you've even gotten to the meat of my story."

"Oh, there's more?" Kahllah asked with a raised eyebrow.

"With me, there's always more." Magic signaled one of the waitresses to grab another bottle. "Now, where were we?"

As the night wore on, the drinks seemed to flow in an endless river. Kahllah didn't usually drink much, but she allowed herself two glasses of champagne. Audrey, on the other hand, was well on her way to being hammered. Normally Kahllah would've been on her back about being intoxicated in public, but tonight she decided to let her have a good time. They were all having fun, including Kahllah. Magic kept her entertained with the stories he told. She felt increasingly comfortable around him, which was unusual since she was always so guarded. She found him not only charming but quite interesting. It was a good night, though all good things come to an end.

The waitress arrived with yet another bottle of champagne. She was just about to place it in the ice bucket when a hand intercepted it. All eyes in the VIP area turned to see who dared touch what didn't belong to him. He was a handsome man, not quite as attractive as Magic, but still easy on the eyes: brown skin, low-cut hair, and a thin goatee. Diamonds adorned his neck, wrist, and both ears. He was wearing a black leather jacket with two white-winged horses running down the sleeves. Kahllah had seen the jacket in a catalog before; it wasn't cheap.

Hard eyes stared at Magic defiantly as the man popped the cork on the bottle and let champagne spill freely onto the floor. He took a deep swig, wiping the excess from his chin with the back of his hand. "Now that's some good shit," he declared with a smile.

"Fuck are you doing here?" Magic rose to his feet. Kahllah didn't miss the fact that Ben remained seated.

"Well hello to you too, Magic. You greet all your friends like this, or just me?"

"That's a word used too loosely." Magic folded his arms. "This is a private event, Tay. You can't just pop up at my spot like this."

"Magic, you wound me. I'll have you know that I was invited."

"By who?"

Tay's eyes drifted to Ben, who picked that moment to refill his cup with ice.

"You serious?"

"C'mon, Magic," Ben said. "I didn't mean no harm by inviting the homey. We're celebrating our accomplishments, ain't we?"

"Exactly—*our* accomplishments."

A scowl touched Tay's lips. "Oh, I see what this is. I was good enough to do dirt for you, but not good enough to break bread?" He shook his head. "Some niggas never change."

"That's exactly my point," Magic shot back.

Tay's eyes went to the women in the VIP area, lingering on Kahllah. "This your new piece, Magic?"

"I'm not anyone's anything," Kahllah countered.

Tay threw his hands up. "I meant no disrespect. You're just a new face in the circle, that's all. I don't know why I'm surprised. Magic has always had an eye for the finer things in life. That's one of the only useful qualities I've picked up from him." He looked over his shoulder and said, "Ain't that right, baby?"

The woman had been so quiet that none of them had even noticed her standing there, like a curvaceous statue carved from polished onyx. She had high cheekbones and black hair that seemed to meld into the dark flesh of her neck. Her legs stretched for days and disappeared up a formfitting green dress. The slit on it was so high that you didn't have to guess whether or not she was wearing underwear. Like Tay, she was decked in jewels—emeralds, to match the dress. Capping off her outfit was a fox stole that hung loosely over her shoulders. To call the woman gorgeous wouldn't have done her justice.

Kahllah watched Magic's eyes cycle through surprise, hurt, and then anger. There had been or was still something between them, clearly.

"How you been, suga?" the girl asked in a rich Southern accent. Her voice was sweet, like what flowers would sound like if they made sounds.

"I'm good, Sable," Magic said dryly.

"Better than good." Tay motioned around the club. "Our boy is on the come-up."

"Magic always did dream bigger than most," Sable said.

"Niggas who spend all their time with their heads in the clouds tend to miss what's right in front of them." Tay pulled Sable closer. "So, you gonna stand there gawking or offer us a seat at your table?"

"Sorry, Tay, but this section is full. If you like, I can have you set up at one of our tables way in the back and send a few bottles over."

"I got my own bread." Tay pulled a knot of bills from his pocket. "I don't do handouts."

"But you got no problem with hand-me-downs?" Magic cut his eyes at Sable.

"You know what?" Kahllah spoke up. "You can have our seats. We were about to leave anyway. Let's go, Audrey."

"Go? Girl, it's not even eleven o'clock. Let's stay until at least midnight." Audrey snuggled closer to Ben.

"Do what you want, but I'm gone," Kahllah said.

"Aw, baby, we didn't mean to scare you off," Tay teased.

"I don't scare easily. I've got an early day tomorrow."

"At least let me walk you out." Magic placed his hand on the small of Kahllah's back and steered her out of the VIP section. As he passed Tay, he whispered, "Don't be here when I come back."

The temperature had dropped a bit when Kahllah got outside. The chilled air felt good on her skin. Except for a few stragglers lined up by the entrance, the crowd from earlier was gone. She and Magic quietly walked the half block to where she'd parked her car. She could tell that the exchange in the club was still weighing on him. Though tempted to ask about the history between him and the woman, she decided against it. It wasn't her business.

"Sorry about all that back there," Magic finally broke the silence. They were waiting for the parking attendant to bring her car up.

"No need to apologize. Your buddy was a bit of a dick, but you've been a gentleman all night."

"Tay ain't no buddy of mine. He's more like a bad rash that just won't go away. But enough about Tay. When can I see *you* again?"

"Well, if I have any follow-up questions before we

roll out the piece on the grand opening, I'll shoot you an e-mail."

"You know that's not how I meant it."

"I figured, and that's where we're gonna keep it. I had a good time tonight, but I don't believe in mixing business and pleasure. Things like that never end well."

"Then forget the write-up. Let's keep it pleasure. Can I take you out for dinner one of these nights? Maybe a few drinks?"

"Thank you, but no," she said politely.

"What? Am I ugly or something?"

"No, you're actually quite handsome."

"Then you must have a man. I don't know why I thought you didn't. A woman as fine as you must have somebody at home waiting on her."

"Nope, single as a dollar bill."

"Then what is it?"

Kahllah searched for the right words. "Let's just say I'm not exactly the kind of girl you take home to your mother."

The valet pulled up with her car. He got out and held the door for Kahllah. She slid fluidly behind the wheel.

"Kahllah, we've all got a past of some sort. Hell, I just laid all my skeletons out for you. I think you'll find that I'm more understanding than you're giving me credit for. Give me one shot, and if you're not feeling me, then I'm out of your hair forever. What harm could it do?"

"More than you know. Goodnight, Magic." She pulled into traffic.

Reentering Voodoo, Magic's butterflies passed and it was back to the matter at hand. Tay knew what he was doing, showing up here. Throwing the fact that he was fucking Sable in his face was just to pour salt in the wound. Magic wasn't dumb; he knew the two of them were an item now, but it had been out of sight, out of mind. He and Sable were ancient history, and whoever she chose to fuck was her business, but seeing them together made him want to punch both of them in the face. He'd told Tay to be gone, yet there was a part of him that hoped the dude had stuck around to spite him. Magic was spoiling for a fight. Much to his disappointment, and relief, when he got back to the VIP area Tay and Sable were nowhere to be found.

Ben greeted him: "Man, for as long as your ass was gone, I thought you decided to slide with shorty." He was still sitting in the same spot, with Audrey up under him.

"Can I borrow him for a minute?" Magic asked Audrey.

"Sure, I need to use the little girls' room anyhow." She got up.

"Don't keep that ass away too long." Ben slapped it as she was walking off, then turned to Magic. "What's good?"

"You tell me. What in God's name would make you think it was a good idea to invite that muthafucka Tay to the grand opening?" Magic was livid.

"You still on that? C'mon, man. I know you guys got some unresolved issues over him fucking with Sable now, but—"

"But shit! This ain't got nothing to do with Sable. This is about Tay being as hot as a firecracker right now after that clusterfuck of a job! Do you know what this looks like?"

"Yeah, it looks like we don't abandon our own when shit gets a little hectic," Ben responded. "Regardless of what's going on, Tay is still one of us."

"Tay is a walking lightning rod, and I don't want us to get hit when it strikes."

"Okay, Magic." Ben put up his hands. "You don't want Tay around the club. I get that. My bad. Still, I think it's a bad idea to cut him off completely when he can still be of use to us."

"Tay can't do shit for me but keep his distance. At this point he's a liability, and anyone associated with him is likely to be a casualty of what's coming his way. We got too much riding to go down with the ship."

"I can dig it. I was just thinking—"

"Like a nigga who could be tempted to do something reckless." There was an icy chill to Magic's voice. "Ben, you know the game can't be played with one foot in and one foot out. If you got aspirations to do some moonlighting, there's the door." He pointed at the exit.

"Magic, I know how hard you've worked to clean up your image. You even brought me in and let me eat with you. Why would I do anything to fuck it up?"

"That's what I'm trying to figure out," Magic said sharply. "I've bled for this shit here, Ben. Put it all on the line to see my dream come true, and I'd do anything to keep it intact, even if it means taking out one of my own."

"That a threat?"

"Only to those who threaten what I've built. Feel me? Ben, you're a loyal dude, and that's one of the things I love about you, but don't let that make you blind to the bigger picture."

"And what is the *bigger picture*, Magic?"

Magic's eyes drifted across the room. He spotted Chancellor King huddled in the shadows by the bar, staring at him. "Survival."

CHAPTER 9

The next day was a drag, and Kahllah settled into bed very early. All she wanted was blissful sleep. It didn't happen. The moment she closed her eyes, she was plagued by a recurring nightmare that she hadn't had in years.

She was a girl again, barely into her teens and still an initiate in the Brotherhood of Blood. Most initiates were given to the Brotherhood before hitting puberty, but she'd entered slightly older. This was back before she inherited her floral calling card, and wore a simple mask of black plaster, same as her peers. During that period, Kahllah had still been struggling to find herself. She'd entered the Brotherhood with two strikes against her. The first was being a legacy, as her adopted father, Priest, was already a member; the second was being female. Traditionally, members of the Brotherhood were male. In all her years with the Order, she had only ever known two other women to serve. This meant that she had to work twice as hard to prove that she belonged, and most times even that wasn't good enough. No matter how hard she tried, she was always reminded that her gender made her lesser. Priest would urge her to stay focused and not to feed into what the others said, but it did little to ease Kahllah's mounting frustrations over unfair treatment.

One day these frustrations came to a boil, and that was when everything changed for her. She was participating in an afternoon sparring class with some of the boys. Their weapons: kendo swords. They were bamboo and hardly lethal, but could still inflict a good amount of damage if you hit your opponent the right way. Their instructor for the day was a woman code-named Tiger Lily. She was a legend within the halls of the Order and one of its most highly decorated members. In the beginning Kahllah had idolized Lily, going out of her way to earn her approval, but the woman couldn't seem to stand the young girl, for reasons that Kahllah wouldn't discover until years later. The sparring match would be her opportunity to finally earn the respect of the elder assassin.

Kahllah had always been gifted in swordplay. She dispatched the first two boys set against her swiftly and efficiently, showcasing a broad array of parries, thrusts, and slashes. Neither opponent lasted more than a minute, and the second even managed to get his wrist broken when he clumsily tried to block her strike. She finished her little display by twirling her wooden sword and taking up a defensive stance. From behind her black mask, her eyes washed over the initiates in attendance as if daring one of them to step up next.

"Well done, little *bruja,*" Tiger Lily said in her thick Spanish accent. Kahllah had made it very clear that she hated that nickname. Wearing no mask that day, Lily allowed them a rare glimpse of her face. She was older and very attractive, with long black hair just starting to gray. Her skin was smooth and tanned, as if she spent her days basking in the sun instead of toiling in the stronghold under the mountain with the rest of them. Hanging from the custom belt at her waist were two metallic tiger claws. Kahllah had heard plenty of stories about the damage these claws could inflict, and could only imagine what her victims must've felt when they fell to their cold touch.

"The Order and my faith have made me strong," Kahllah said. "My weapon is an extension of my very soul, and will always strike true when in service of my Order."

"I've seen better," Lily said dismissively, and began walking away.

"If there are any who claim to be better than me, let them come forward, no matter their level or rank."

Lily turned abruptly and gave her a crooked grin.

She grabbed one of the practice swords off the wall and tossed it to Kahllah. "How well will you do when you're not swinging a broomstick?"

The young man Lily put her against next was tall and as thin as a wisp. A black glove covered his left hand. While most initiates of the Order were forced to wear the same black masks, his was white with a golden palm carved into the center. The fact that he had already earned his totem spoke to his skill, though his legend had been whispered in the dorms even before he had arrived. Back then Kahllah had known him as Seven-Palms. It was a moniker he had earned because of his lethal hands. It was said that Seven-Palms was so fast that he could land seven blows in the time it took others to launch one. He had been away the last three years, studying under Brotherhood elders around the globe. He'd only come to the mountain stronghold at Lily's request, to serve as her apprentice. Kahllah had always hoped that the honor would fall to her, and the fact that it had been handed to an outsider created a resentment in her toward a boy she hardly knew.

"You may want to arm yourself," Kahllah said, noticing that Seven-Palms hadn't picked up a sword.

"No need. I want to feel the softness of your body with my own hands before I break it." His reply added fuel to the already-building fire in Kahllah's gut. Like his mentor, he wasn't taking her seriously. She'd make him regret this.

Kahllah and Seven-Palms moved around each other in a circle, each assessing the other for weak points. He kept his fighting stance loose, one arm tucked back and ready to fire.

"Are you two going to dance or fight?" Tiger Lily taunted. "Come on, little *bruja!*"

Tired of hearing the elder's mouth, Kahllah decided it was time to close it. Her strike was as swift as the wind, but Seven-Palms moved at a speed that seemed almost unnatural. Twice Kahllah found herself hacking at the air. On her next attempt, Seven-Palms knocked her off-balance and struck the back of her head. It felt like being hit with a lead pipe; the force made spots dance before her eyes. She retaliated with a series of combinations that got him to backpedal. When she had him off-balance, she jabbed the blade at his face, intent on blinding him. At the last moment, he raised his gloved hand. Kahllah expected to see the blade split his palm, but instead it stopped as if it had struck a wall, sending a shock wave through the sword and her arm. It made sense now: Seven-Palms didn't need a weapon because he *was* a weapon.

In her studies, Kahllah had come across old scrolls that told of the discipline Seven-Palms was using. It was called pugilism—a technique that hardened 99 percent of the skin, making it resistant to most blades. She'd thought that the technique was just a myth, written into the Brotherhood scrolls to add to their legend, but Seven-Palms was proof that it was quite real.

Kahllah came at him in a whirlwind of slashes and jabs. She landed several good blows, but the blade seemed to have little to no effect. If she planned to beat him, she needed to break his discipline, which meant finding that one percent of flesh that hadn't been hardened. It would act as a kill switch. But her arms began to tire, and she could feel herself getting winded. Kahllah figured she was as good as beaten. It was then that she picked up on something. Every time she swung at Seven-Palms, there was one part of his body that he made sure to protect: the crook of his arm, near where his elbow and bicep connected. It was a long shot, but it was all she had.

Kahllah faked like she was going to cut him high and then diverted her strike to the area she'd pinpointed. The tip of the blade stuck his skin. At first there was nothing . . . then a small red stain appeared on his shirt. She had found it! Seeing his own blood made Seven-Palms's focus slip, and his next few swings were wild and angry. The initiates who had been quietly watching the match were now chattering away, in awe of the epic battle. This may have been only a sparring match to them, but Kahllah was trying to make a statement.

Seven-Palms fired a punch at Kahllah that, had she not dodged at the last second, would've broken her jaw, if not taken her head off her shoulders. He was playing for keeps. Moving more off instinct than thought, Kahllah whirled, bringing her blade down with everything she had. The practice sword bit into his arm with a sickening sound. It tore messily through skin and muscle, only pausing upon striking bone. Completely in a frenzy now, she yanked the blade free and somehow cut him again, this time across a leg, dropping him to one knee.

Tiger Lily called for her to stand down, but Kahllah was too far gone to hear anything but the blood pumping in her own ears. Beating Lily's toy wasn't enough—she intended to break it. She honed in on the exposed flesh of his throat and struck.

Seven-Palms would've lost his head that day had fate not intervened. Tiger Lily suddenly appeared between them. Her iron claws grasped the tip of Kahllah's blade. Kahllah tried to yank it free, but the older woman's grip was unyielding.

"I said enough!" Lily barked. "This is a sparring match, not mortal combat. You almost killed your brother."

"And I would've, had his wet nurse not come to his rescue," Kahllah growled, her adrenaline still pumping.

Tiger Lily released the sword and shook her head sadly. "You are good, Lotus, but you will never be great. You lack the focus that is required of those who serve the Order."

"Is it that I lack focus or that my presence here makes you insecure?" Kahllah challenged, immediately regretting her words. She'd spoken more out of anger than actually wanting to challenge Tiger Lily, but the gauntlet had been laid.

Lily's response was quiet but immediate—she sliced Kahllah across the gut with her claws. The talons were so sharp, Kahllah didn't even realize she'd been cut until she looked down and saw the trails of red across her stomach. She raised her sword to try and mount a defense, but the cheap metal was no match for Tiger Lily's custom claws. The blade broke in half and left her defenseless.

"Little *bruja*," she flexed her claws, "I'm going to make you scream."

Tiger Lily held true to her word. Kahllah no longer had to wonder what victims of those claws felt, because she found out firsthand. For the first time in ages, Kahllah screamed.

CHAPTER 10

"Kahllah . . . Kahllah!" She was pulled from her nightmare by someone shouting her name. Her brain was still half-asleep, but when she felt a pair of hands on her shoulders, her reflexes did what came naturally. Kahllah slapped the hands away and shot out her palms.

"Fuck!" someone shouted, followed by the sound of something breaking.

Her head whipped around, heart beating rapidly. It took a few seconds for Kahllah to realize that she was in someone's bedroom and not the sparring room. Phantom burns ran down her stomach and back, where the claws had left scars that she still carried. That was a day she'd never forget; Tiger Lily had seen to that. She never saw Seven-Palms again. Infection had set in on the wound she gave him and he lost the use of his arm. In her attempt to spite Tiger Lily, she had ruined his chances of advancing in the Brotherhood. Nobody wanted a one-armed assassin. What she'd done to him was the one thing she regretted about that day.

The voice drew her attention. "Is it safe for me to get up now?" She had been trapped so firmly in her dream that she'd forgotten she wasn't alone—she was, in fact, in his Harlem apartment. His six-foot, naked frame was crammed in the corner at an awkward angle. He was bleeding from a thin cut on his forearm, from the glass candleholder he had broken during his fall after she'd struck him.

"Dominic!" Kahllah gasped.

Dominic was her little secret. She had met him while digging into the Jerome Yates case. Dominic was one of the attorneys who'd been working to get him released from prison. Their common crusade to seek justice for Jerome had them spending a lot of time together. She couldn't remember how many late nights they'd spent going over his case files. Dominic had been fresh out of law school, hungry and eager to champion the wrongly convicted. Kahllah reasoned that was what had attracted her to him, his passion. She couldn't recall when it turned sexual. It was like something that had always existed between them, instead of a wine-fueled late night where both of them had some stress they needed to get out. It felt good, so why stop? A commitment would've complicated things, so they kept it what it was, a booty call.

"Sleeping with you is getting more and more dangerous, you know." Dominic pulled himself back onto the bed. He was athletically built, and worked out a few times a week. A tribal tattoo snaked across his well-defined bicep. Though not quite chocolate, he was too dark to be considered light skinned. His chin was covered by a fine stubble that wouldn't grow much past that point; it hadn't in the time she'd known him, which sometimes felt like forever.

"I'm sorry, Dominic. I was having—"

"I know, a nightmare," he cut her off. "I've been watching you sleep long enough to know when it's fitful. From the way you were screaming, it must've been intense."

"You have no idea." Kahllah ran her hand over her T-shirt, feeling the scars beneath.

"Then give me an idea. K, I know we agreed to keep this thing casual, but that doesn't mean I'm not here if you ever need to talk."

"And what makes you think I need to talk?"

"Maybe the fact that you're fighting in your sleep every time we spend the night together; or the fact that, in the months since we've been seeing each other, you've never taken your shirt off in front of me. You got a third boob you're trying to hide?" He reached for her shirt and she reflexively jerked back. "See what I mean? Kahllah, your actions speak of somebody who has clearly been hurt in her life. That's a lot of baggage to carry around. Let somebody else help you with that load."

"I thought the only loads we were worried about were the ones let go between our legs." Kahllah rolled off the bed and headed to Dominic's closet, where she kept some clothes. She pulled out a pair of sweats and sneakers.

"Whenever I try and figure out what's going on with you, you either make a joke, change the subject, or run off. I'm getting two out of three tonight, huh?"

Kahllah paused her dressing and looked at Dominic. She wished she could say that she blamed him. The harder he tried, the farther she pushed him away. "I know you probably think I'm being a world-class bitch, but my history is complicated. How can I put something into words that I'm still trying to process myself?"

"So, what, I'm supposed to just sit by and watch you suffer through whatever you're dealing with and not feel in a way about it?"

"I'd think less of you if you didn't worry, and I'm thankful. Truly, I am. But I got this." Kahllah pulled on her hoodie. "I'm about to go for a run."

"Why can't you just let me in?"

"Because not every cause is yours to champion," she replied flatly.

* * *

For early evening, there were surprisingly few people on the streets, which Kahllah was happy about. She had no direction; she just wanted to run and think. Jogging gave her the space to clear her head.

She hated to be cold to Dominic, but it was a necessary evil. Though they had agreed to keep things loose, she knew he was starting to get attached. She'd be lying if she said she didn't have strong feelings for him, but she knew that pursuing a relationship wasn't even a remote possibility. Kahllah had done a great bit of wrong in her years of service to the Brotherhood. There were people who would love to find a way to hurt her, which was why she stayed clear of attachments. Dominic would be kept at arm's length just like everything else she cared about.

As she jogged, she thought about how screwed up her head had been since she'd seen the pictures of that van. When she glimpsed those claw marks, it brought back memories buried in the deepest parts of her mind. There was only one person she knew who wielded claws able to do that kind of damage: Tiger Lily. But the old hag had been dead for years, or so it had been reported. Tiger Lily had been branded a traitor when it was discovered that she'd been stealing Brotherhood technology and selling it on the black market to the highest bidders. She had supposedly been killed while trying to orchestrate a rebellion in some developing South American country. Kahllah would never wish death on another member of the Order, but she couldn't say that she was unhappy when she got word of Lily's passing. It was more likely that this was some copycat rather than Kahllah's past coming back to haunt her. She tried to remind herself that what had happened to those people in that van wasn't her business, but she was having trouble shaking it.

She shifted her thoughts to the life she was leading now and the people in it. Magic had left quite the impression. He was ambitious, as well as good looking. That ability to captivate a room would take him further than a pistol ever would. She had to admit, it had been flattering when he kept trying to press her into a date. Not that she'd ever seriously consider dating him. Dominic was square for the most part, and she still had trouble dealing with him, so she could only imagine what getting involved with someone like Magic would be like. Despite all his charms, Magic was as crooked as the letter *S*.

She didn't doubt his sincerity—in what he had gone through, in what he was trying to accomplish—but she also knew there was more to him than he let on. Like her, Magic wore two faces. She had suspected it from the beginning, but what confirmed it was his interaction with Tay and Sable.

Tay made no secret about what he was—a criminal.

He wore it like a badge of honor. Though Magic tried to downplay his relationship with Tay, the tension between them didn't smell of an old grudge. Whatever was going on was fresh, and, she suspected, deeper than both of them having slept with the same woman. Ultimately, however, it was none of her business. She was there to get what she needed for the magazine. Nothing more. Her days of playing detective were over.

Kahllah had been so locked in, she didn't even realize she had jogged all the way to her office until she looked up and saw the bodega she got her breakfast from in the morning. She was about to turn around and start heading back when something caught her eye. She thought she saw what looked like the beam of a flashlight coming through her office window. The only people who had keys were Audrey and herself. With it being the weekend, she doubted it was Audrey.

Kahllah knelt and removed a flat blade from the sole of her sneaker—she kept it there in case of emergencies. It was no thicker than a box cutter, but sturdy and with a ring on the end just big enough to slide your finger through. Now armed, she moved toward her office. She didn't bother calling the police—that would come after she dealt with whoever had been desperate or dumb enough to break into her space.

The inside of *Real Talk* was dark, so it wasn't hard to

spot the sole source of light, which was coming from her personal office. The door was open and she could hear what sounded like the flipping of pages. The alarms hadn't been tripped . . . Could it actually be Audrey?

She kept to the shadows, blade secured around her finger. Her heart raced faster as she approached. She rolled into the room, flicking on the light, ready to pounce. She expected to find a burglar, but instead found a cop.

"Wolf?"

The detective sat comfortably behind Kahllah's desk, thumbing through one of her files. "You know, for somebody with so many secrets, you'd think you would've invested in a better security system."

"What the fuck are you doing in my office?" It had been months since she'd last seen or heard from Wolf.

"Reaching out to an old friend."

"You could've used the phone or sent an e-mail like a normal person." She snatched the file from him.

"Better this way, so I can look you in the eyes while I speak my piece." Wolf's voice was devoid of the warmth it had had last time. "Can you account for your whereabouts from around six to six thirty yesterday evening?"

"Why do I feel like I'm being interrogated?" Kahllah folded her arms.

"How you answer will determine that. Where were you?"

"I was getting ready for work. My magazine is covering the grand opening of a place called Voodoo. I went there with Audrey to interview the owner, a guy named Magic. I stayed for a couple of hours, then went home at about ten or so." She paused. "Wolf, what is this about?"

After a long pause he said, "A dead cop." He slid his cell phone across the table so she could see a picture from the crime scene.

Kahllah couldn't hide the surprise on her face. "*Sweet thang*," she whispered, remembering the encounter she'd had with the cop. Though at that time half of his head wasn't missing.

"Can I take the look on your face as confirmation that you knew the victim?"

"Not exactly. We bumped into each other at a restaurant yesterday. I'd never seen him before that. Why are you asking me about—" She stopped short. "Wait, you think I did this?"

"Would I be that far off? Pegging you for a killer, I mean?"

Kahllah remained silent.

"Okay, let's try it this way." Wolf dug into his pocket and produced the baggie he'd gotten from Lieutenant

Tasha Grady and tossed it onto the desk. "This was found at the crime scene."

"Impossible!" It was a black lotus, her calling card. Lotuses weren't naturally black, but Kahllah had figured out a way to change the genetic makeup of the seeds through crossbreeding. It was a technique she'd learned from an elder of the Brotherhood who had since passed on. She examined the baggie to check the authenticity of the flower. It had to be a replica . . . But no, it was one of her crossbreeds. "This doesn't make sense."

"That's what I've been trying to tell myself all night."

"Then you should listen to yourself, because this isn't the work of the Black Lotus. Think about it, Wolf. This man was shot. In all the Black Lotus crime scenes you've investigated, were any of the victims shot?"

"Assassins adapt as needed, at least the good ones do. Last time I checked, the Black Lotus was one of the best."

"Which is why the Lotus wouldn't have been involved with a mess like this. There's no . . ."

"Honor in it," Wolf finished her sentence, recalling what he had been trying to explain to Grady. "For as much as I'd like to take you at your word, you can't deny how strong the evidence is against you. If you're as innocent as you say, then you shouldn't mind coming back to the station with me to clear your name."

"I think we both know that I can't do that."

"Let's not make this any harder." He tossed his cuffs on the desk. "Now why don't you do us both a favor and slip those on?"

"The hell I will! I'm being framed! Somebody is out there killing in the name of the Black Lotus, and I need to find out who it is."

"Your vigilante days are over, little lady." Wolf drew his gun and pointed it at her. "I'd rather not do this the hard way."

"Are you serious?" Kahllah took a step forward and Wolf tightened his grip on the weapon.

"That's far enough. We've danced in close quarters before and it didn't turn out good for me, remember? I'm going to need some distance until those lethal hands of yours are nice and secured by those bracelets. Please, don't make me ask you again."

"You are making a mistake." Kahllah picked up the cuffs and secured one to each wrist.

"I hope so, Kahllah. I really do."

"This is bullshit!"

"Better it's me bringing you in than one of my colleagues. They're not taking this dead cop development very well. The last thing either of us needs is a bunch of cops full of piss and vinegar trying to take you down. At least with me you'll get a fair shake."

"Am I supposed to find comfort somewhere in that?"

"Listen, don't shoot the messenger. I'm just doing my job. We've all got a part to play."

"I know, and that's why I'm hoping you'll understand." And then she acted.

Wolf's brain registered the warning a split second too late. As deftly as a magician, Kahllah had freed her hands of the cuffs and turned on Wolf. She grabbed his wrist with one hand, and used the other to slide a cuff inside the trigger guard, preventing him from being able to pull it. Wolf tried to grab Kahllah's hair but got elbowed in the nose. They fought for control of the gun like a couple waltzing. He'd forgotten how strong she was but was reminded when she hugged his thighs, lifted him off his feet, and rammed him against the window. He felt the glass shatter, followed by a rush of wind and then pain.

The hood of a car broke his fall. He was seeing stars and couldn't catch his breath. One of his ribs was probably cracked. He looked around for Kahllah, but she was gone, of course. He had no plans to report the incident and get the department involved. As Grady had said, this was personal. There was no doubt in his mind that she could've killed him if she wanted to, but she had spared his life . . . again. Hardly the actions of a guilty person. Still, he had a job to do. He just hoped that she could find the real killer before the detective found *her*. The hunt was on.

CHAPTER 11

Something about sitting in the oversize wingback chair made Tay feel royal. It was tall and upholstered in soft purple velvet, with gold buttons running down the seams. It was a welcome change from the cheap furniture he'd been used to. He could remember summer days of sitting in a project apartment with no air-conditioning, trying to keep his legs from sticking to the plastic covers that his grandmother refused to take off the couch. Those were some tough times, but they were now in his rearview. The only thing he was focused on was his future, which was looking pretty good from where he was sitting.

Sable was standing across the room in front of a full-length mirror, wearing nothing but sheer black lingerie. For the past half hour she had been trying on the new clothes that Tay had bought for her. Tay didn't mind. Watching Sable was one of his favorite pastimes. Sometimes he'd just stare at her, wondering how he had been lucky enough to land a woman as fine as this. Then he would always remind himself that luck had nothing to do with it. This was a case of the better man winning, even if the race had been fixed.

Tay had known Sable longer than Magic had. Indeed, it was Tay who had introduced them, which was one of his biggest regrets. She was from his neighborhood, had moved to New York from Dallas right before the start of freshman year. Back then she wasn't quite so poised. She was a dusty country girl with no real sense of fashion, and self-esteem that was in the toilet. That changed when Tay took her under his wing. His hustle was boosting from department stores and reselling the stuff on the block for half price, and Sable became his accomplice. To Tay's surprise, the seemingly innocent girl was a natural thief. She could hit a store and trim it of a few grand's worth of merchandise before anyone even realized she was inside. Tay and Sable were like the Bonnie and Clyde of shoplifters. Sable showed no less skill and enthusiasm when their hustle switched from boosting to strong-arm robbery.

This was about the time Magic came into the picture. Magic wasn't much older than Tay, but he was already deep in the robbery game. He'd come up under two older dudes named Archie and Butch, notorious stickup kids. Whenever Tay caught a lick at a department store, he would bring the items to Magic and his crew first, knowing they were going to spend big. It was

Magic who convinced Tay to stop throwing stones at the penitentiary for nickels and try something more rewarding. Of course, when Tay got down with Magic's crew, Sable came along for the ride. That was the beginning of the end.

Tay should've known from the way Sable and Magic looked at each other the first time they met that he was setting himself up for disaster. Tay never hid his feelings for Sable. They had fooled around a little bit back when they were still boosting, but it wasn't anything major. Sable always seemed hesitant to take the next step, as if waiting for something bigger. With Magic she didn't have to wait very long. So Magic was in and Tay was out.

Tay always carried some resentment for the couple. He felt like it should've been him instead of Magic with that onyx goddess on his arm. Tay kept his game face when it came to getting money, but the thought of them together ate at him. He'd even gone as far as trying to get with Sable behind Magic's back. Although she'd shut him down, the fact that she never mentioned it to Magic gave Tay hope. More hope came in the form of a dirty secret that Tay used to drive a wedge between them.

As a teenager, Sable had been quiet and shy, but when she finally came out of her shell she'd grown into a party girl of sorts. She became a regular on the club circuit, indulging in whatever vices were at her disposal, including cocaine. It started out as just chipping, doing a few lines here and there at parties, but gradually the monkey on Sable's back began to grow. Magic was oblivious because he thought the sun rose and set in Sable's sweet pussy, but Tay was well aware. He sat back and waited for an opportunity to use it to his advantage.

Sable had managed to get caught up in what seemed like a random raid. She was uptown scoring some coke when the police ran in. Unbeknownst to her, she had been the target all along. A month or so prior, she'd made the mistake of pulling a job with some guys who weren't part of their immediate crew. Then one of them got caught and gave Sable up. The police had been on her for weeks. It was her first time arrested, and outside of the snitch's word, they didn't have much on Sable. With a decent lawyer she probably could've gotten off with just probation, but being naive to the law, she allowed the police to spook her into believing she'd go away for a long time—unless she gave them something they could use. She gave them Archie. The two of them had never gotten along, and Magic was the real brains of the crew, so she figured no one would miss the old con. She had no idea that when the police finally caught up with Archie, Magic would be in the car with him.

The secret would've probably gone to the grave with Sable, had it not been for dumb luck: one of Tay's cousins was a clerk in the DA's office. She knew that Sable was part of Tay's crew, so when she saw the girl's case file come through, she immediately told Tay. Most would've exposed Sable's snake move and then left her to her fate, but Tay had a more sinister idea. He confronted Sable about what she'd done and threatened to expose her unless she broke things off with Magic and became *his*. Sable found herself in a pinch. She could come clean to Magic—explain the whole situation and hope that he loved her enough to understand. It was a long shot, yet he would maybe find it in his heart to forgive her. But there was no way Butch was going to let her off. He was raised in an era where if you snitched, you died. Tay had put Sable in a lose-lose situation. So she chose her life over her heart.

The story Sable fed Magic was one that Tay had insisted on: With Magic spending all his time chasing his dream of becoming legit, she had started to feel neglected. She had fallen out of love with him and developed feelings for Tay. The look of hurt in his eyes rocked her to the core. She hated herself for it, but Tay had left her no choice.

Everyone had expected Magic to go through the roof, but he took it surprisingly well. Naturally he was angry at what had happened right under his nose, but in typical Magic fashion he blamed himself for mixing business with pleasure and chalked it up to the game, rather than admitting that he had been bested. Butch, on the other hand, wasn't so accepting. He wanted to kill both Sable and Tay, or at the very least boot them from the crew, but Magic wouldn't allow it. Their crew was making a lot of money, and Tay and Sable played a big part in that. "I'll never let my heart or a bitch affect our bottom line," was all Magic would say. This never sat quite right with Butch, and Tay knew that one day he could be a problem. Which was why he'd had Butch killed while he was out in Pennsylvania last year.

No matter how cool Magic tried to play it, everybody knew that losing Archie and Sable back-to-back had hurt Magic deeply. Tay had pride in his work: Magic had taken Sable from him, and he'd taught Magic the pain of loss in turn. The unexpected blessing was that those back-to-back tragedies were enough to make Magic start to withdraw, allowing Tay to gradually step up. While Magic chased his corporate dreams, Tay was ushering their crew into a new era. The little dude whom Magic used to buy stolen clothes from had taken his bitch and his business. It had all come to him by default, but men like Tay never cared about the means, only the ends.

"I like that one on you," Tay said to Sable as she slipped into a tight black number. She promptly took it off and picked up a different dress. "What? You don't value my opinion?"

"You're a wiz at cracking safes, but you don't have much fashion sense." She looked at his skinny jeans and oversize shoes. Tay was always a year or two late when it came to trends.

"Where you getting all dressed up to go, anyway? I thought we were gonna stay in and order food."

"You can do what you like, Tay. I'm stepping out for drinks with some friends." Sable wiggled into a red dress.

"You don't have any friends."

"Just goes to show that you don't pay attention to what's going on around you."

"What if I said I wanted you to stay here instead?"

"I'd tell you not to wait up." Sable picked up a small baggie of coke from the dresser, shook a bit out onto the back of her hand, and snorted it. After clearing her nostrils, she went to the mirror and began applying lipstick.

Tay got up from the chair and eased up behind her. He pressed himself against her ass so she could feel his erection, and nuzzled the nape of her neck. "Damn, you smell good." He ran his hands up her dress until they reached the zipper. He tried to pull it down, but she stopped him.

"Chill, I told you I'm going out." She stepped out of his reach.

"Yeah, drinks and shit, right? Where y'all going to get drinks, Voodoo?"

Sable stopped with her lipstick and cast him a dirty look. "Ain't nothing in Voodoo for me. You saw to that, remember?"

"You still ain't learned your lesson about running your mouth, huh?" Tay saw the hurt on her face. Good. He wanted to hurt her.

"Fuck you, Tay!" she said over her shoulder.

"Now you're speaking my language." He pulled her in roughly. "You know, you been acting funny over this pussy since we came back from Voodoo. You think I ain't peep game?"

"I'm acting funny because this pussy isn't on call to you 24/7!" Sable shoved him away. "Let's get something straight. Our deal is that I play the role of the girlfriend in public and let you hit it once in a while behind closed doors. I'm not trying to lay up under you and let you go nuts on my pussy like I want to procreate with you. This is an arrangement, so don't slip too deep into whatever script you wrote in your head about what this is supposed to be."

"Who the fuck you talking to?" Tay grabbed her by the arm. "You know, I don't ever hear you talking slick when you're out spending my money!"

"*Our* money. Or have you forgotten that my hands

get as dirty as the rest of y'all?" She let her words linger for a moment before jerking out of his grasp.

"Fuck it, go be a ho in these streets if you want! All you care about is feeding your nose and partying," Tay spat before returning to his seat. Part of him wanted to smack her upside the head for the way she'd been talking to him lately, but the girl was a bull; he'd have to be prepared to knock her out.

As Tay sat there contemplating a way to fuck up Sable's night, someone rang the doorbell. He looked at Sable, waiting for her to answer the door, but she ignored him. "Lazy bitch," he grumbled on his way out of the bedroom. Grabbing his gun from the coffee table in the living room, he took a quick look through the peephole and saw Ben.

"What up?" Ben greeted when he stepped into the apartment. He was wearing dark jeans, a smoke-gray sweater, and a black overcoat. His black leather bowling bag was in his hand. Anybody who knew Ben knew that he hadn't bowled a day in his life, but the bag was never too far out of his reach.

"Trying to keep from going upside this bitch's head," Tay said loud enough for Sable to hear through the open bedroom door. "I should've let Magic keep her."

"Not my business or why I'm here." Ben tolerated the couple but didn't respect what they had done. The only reason he still dealt with them was out of greed. Tay's scores had been lining Ben's pockets for months; as long as he remained useful, Ben would turn a blind eye to his deceit.

"So, what happened with the old man?" Tay got right to it. He had been on edge since he'd seen Magic talking to Chancellor King at Voodoo. It was a bad omen.

Ben shrugged. "Him and Magic chopped it up for a while, then he spent about an hour giving us the side-eye before breaking out."

None of this was new to Tay. He and Sable had played the cut watching Magic and Chancellor whispering like a couple of old maids. Tay didn't have to hear anything to know what the topic of conversation was. "How much do you think he knows?"

"Enough to bring him into Voodoo asking questions, but not enough to where you and me are chatting at the bottom of the Hudson right now."

"What about Magic? Where does he stand on all this?"

"Where he always does: out of the way. So long as what we got going on doesn't interfere with what he's got going on, Magic will look away. But as soon as the two start to overlap, there's a problem."

"I ain't worried about Magic."

"Then that makes you dumber than I thought. Magic

might've let you get away with fucking his bitch, but I doubt he'll be so forgiving if you fuck his business. The lack of respect you showed at Voodoo didn't earn you any favor either."

"What you mean? I was just coming to support my old friend's new endeavor."

"Bullshit! I invited you because I thought him seeing you there to celebrate the moment with us would be a show of good faith and a way to wash away some of the bad blood between you two. But you had to bring your bitch and rub his nose in it, didn't you?"

"What's the use of having nice things if you can't show them off?"

"You and Sable can play with fire all you want, but don't burn me in the process," Ben said. "Magic's got a long memory, and he never forgets a slight."

"What's he gonna do, slap me on the wrist again?" The fact that Magic had let him take Sable with no real repercussions made him feel that Magic was weak.

"You don't get it, do you? Magic isn't the type of dude who wears his emotions on his sleeve. He's like a viper, laying in the cut until the right moment—and then strikes!" Ben slammed his fist into his hand for emphasis. "Seeing the two of you at the club has him worked up about the heat that could come down on him for what you did."

"Don't you mean what *we* did?"

"Don't play word games with me, Tay. You get the point. Magic is no fool, and you should know that. There will be consequences behind this shit. I was able to spin him, but I think he's still suspicious."

"Magic has always been suspicious. Nothing new. Besides, if he jumps out the window and makes a move, it could jeopardize that squeaky-clean image he's trying so hard to maintain."

"Just because Magic is doing the club thing now doesn't mean he ain't still got some dog in him. You and I both know what he's capable of when his back is against the wall. You keep poking that bear, you're going to get the claws. I can promise you that."

"Whatever you say." Tay was able to use Ben's love of money to lure him into their capers, but there was never any question as to where his loyalties lay. He was like a faithful dog at its master's feet. When the time came, Tay would get rid of Ben, but at the moment he still needed him. "Anyway, our friends reached out earlier."

By *friends*, Tay meant the people who supplied their crew with high-tech weaponry, in exchange for giving up a cut of their profits and taking on the occasional contract. Tay had been introduced to them through Magic. When he took over the crew, he feared they would no longer receive the weapons, but fortunately their benefactors were more loyal to profit than they were to Magic. Business continued as usual. The unique weapons had been a game changer, and thanks to them, Tay and his crew were well on their way to sitting at the top of the food chain.

"What's the word?" Ben asked anxiously.

"Timetable has changed. We're moving on the spot tonight."

"Tonight?" The job in question wasn't supposed to go down until the following week at the earliest.

"Seems they've gotten a little anxious and want to speed things up."

"I don't like this, man. Changing the plan suddenly like this feels a little suspect."

"I don't like it either. I would've told them no, had they not agreed to double our normal fee."

Ben whistled. "That's a lot of bread to bust into some meth lab."

"It ain't meth they're cooking in there. It's supposed to be some new shit, hasn't even hit the streets yet."

"So, we taking the shit?" Ben asked.

"Nah, no heavy lifting this time. All we gotta do is snatch the recipe they're using to make it, which is on a laptop hard drive. It'll be the easiest score we've had in months."

"You're planning another job?" Sable startled the

men. They hadn't even noticed her come out of the bedroom.

"Same job, different time frame." Tay repeated the explanation for Sable.

"Tay, don't you think that after what happened yesterday we might wanna consider slowing down for a minute?" Seeing the corpses in the van had spooked Sable. She was a thief, and murder was out of her depth. Her ear had been to the streets; apparently bounties had been placed on the heads of those involved with the deaths of the newlyweds. They hadn't been the killers, but they would be hard pressed to prove it.

"Baby, this ain't no time to be getting cold feet. We all feeling some type of way about what happened, but it don't change the fact that we got other obligations. You wanna keep those pretty claws you've become so fond of, then we need to keep up with our quota." She still didn't look convinced. "Listen, sweetness, I'll make a deal with you. After we pull this quick snatch, we'll take some time off."

Sable glared at him.

"Scout's honor." Tay raised his fingers in mock salute. "Once we hit this lab tonight, we'll have plenty of cash. You and me can go spend a few weeks somewhere warm until all this blows over."

Sable knew that everything coming out of his mouth

was bullshit, but she was used to it by now. When Tay first took over, he had shown promise as a leader, but lately he'd been slacking. When Magic was running things, what had endeared him to the rest of them was that he always put the needs of the crew before his own. Tay was too blinded by his own ambition to see what was good for anybody besides himself. She feared that one day he would be all their undoing. Times like these were when she missed her former lover the most. She couldn't help but wonder if she'd have been better off risking Magic's wrath for snitching rather than locking herself into this facade with Tay. "I'll be back later." She grabbed her coat and went out the door.

"You mean what you said?" Ben asked after Sable had gone.

"About what?"

"Stepping off after this next job."

Tay shrugged. "I dunno. Sable seems a little on the fragile side lately. Maybe I'm putting too much on her and the downtime will do her some good."

"Downtime? Nigga, this ain't no regular nine-to-five. We criminals, remember? You're the only one with a direct connection to our benefactor, and I can't afford a hiatus while you and your shorty go on a couple's retreat. You wanna go soak up some sun, then I'm gonna need a face-to-face with the benefactor so I'm not left hanging."

"You know that's not how this works. He ain't gonna go for me bringing nobody new to see him."

"I ain't new! I been a part of this crew for longer than you have."

"Yet it was me who Magic brought in to meet his guy," Tay reminded him. He could tell from the way Ben's eye twitched that the remark had stung. Good, he'd intended it to. Magic had fucked up by letting Tay get too close to the people backing him. This was a mistake that he didn't plan to make with Ben. Still, he needed the big man to play nice for now, so he tossed him a bone. "Listen, once all this blows over, you got my word that I'll introduce you," he lied. "In the meantime, while Sable and me are gone, I'll set up a few nice scores that you and Snake can take off."

"Cobb!" Ben snorted. He couldn't stand working with the detective, but Tay refused to get rid of him. He figured having a cop in the fold would give them an advantage. Ben saw the logic, but would never be comfortable working with the police in any capacity. "You see him today?"

"No, I haven't. I've been trying to get him on the phone all day, but nothing."

"Maybe after what happened he's had a change of heart and gone back to the right side of the law. I don't trust that pig."

"The thought has crossed my mind too, but Frank is more criminal than he is cop. He's getting money, so it wouldn't make sense to double-cross us. He's probably laid up somewhere high as a kite with some bitch."

"You willing to bet your freedom on that?" Ben asked.

Tay was not. "You've got a point. Why don't you pay our little friend a visit before the job and make sure he hasn't forgotten which side his bread is buttered on."

"With pleasure." Ben grinned and patted his bowling bag.

PART III

PREY

CHAPTER 12

K ahllah sat behind the wheel of the Honda Civic, trying her best to suppress her mounting agitation. The car was filthy: fast-food wrappers littered the floor, stains marked the seats, and everything reeked of cigarette smoke. She, a clean freak, would never keep her car in such a condition, but this vehicle wasn't hers. She had appropriated it in a haste because she needed a quick getaway. She didn't have to worry about its owner reporting it stolen, because he was secured in the trunk. He wasn't dead, just unconscious. His fault for trying to play hero when she was stealing the car. So long as he didn't give her any more trouble, he would not taste her blade. The kiss of steel was reserved for another.

She still couldn't believe the evening's turn of events. Someone was trying to hang a body on her. This wasn't the first time someone had taken a life in the name of the Black Lotus. She had become notorious in New York underworld circles as of late and birthed a number of copycat killers. Mostly they were nutjobs in masks, trying to score a payday, hardly worth her attention. But this one was different. She still wasn't sure how the killer had managed to get ahold of one of her crossbred flowers, but she was going to take great pleasure in finding out.

Before she could begin her investigation, she needed a change of clothes. She was still wearing the sweats and running shoes she'd put on when she left Dom's apartment. There was no way she could risk going back there with Wolf looking for her. She drove the stolen car into Midtown, where she was renting yet another storage unit under a fake name. The one in the Bronx was mostly used for files, but the Midtown unit was where she kept a spare set of her *tools of the trade*.

She slipped into a black jumpsuit, combat boots, and a thin Kevlar vest, which she covered with a black long-sleeved shirt. She tossed her spare mask into the duffel that carried her weapons for the night, including several stilettos and a short sword.

To clear her name, she needed to find Detective Cobb's real killer, which would be tricky since she didn't have a whole lot to go on. She figured her best lead would be tracking down the man she had seen him meeting with at Amy Ruth's. Sully Roth proved easy enough to find. Because of his conviction, he had to register as a sex offender upon his release from prison. A quick web search led her to his current address. It was a two-story house in Bensonhurst that he shared with his mom, a far cry from the high-rise apartment where he had once tried to rape Kahllah.

She didn't have to wait long for the worm to show himself. About an hour into her surveillance of the house, Roth showed up driving a brown beater. From the way his head kept whipping around when he got out, she could tell that he was nervous. It was like he feared the devil was hiding behind one of the bushes surrounding his abode, instead of in a stolen car across the street. He went inside and came back out less than two minutes later, tossing a bag onto the passenger seat before rushing back into the house, leaving the front door slightly ajar. From the look of it, he was preparing for a trip. She could've taken him right then and there, but figured she would let him leave and then follow in hopes that he would lead her to whoever else may have been involved. Fifteen minutes or so went by. Maybe he had changed his mind about running, or decided to postpone the trip—but he'd left his car door wide open. Doing so in this city was like begging for your wheels to be stolen. Something was wrong.

She strapped on the harness that held her blades before getting out of the car. She crept across the street, head on swivel for police or any potential witnesses. A woman dressed in all black and wearing a mask was likely to draw attention. Thankfully no one was about.

Pressing herself against the side of the house, she peered in through the living room window. A small television sat on a wooden stool, turned to a game show. At first all seemed normal, but then she spotted something: a furry slipper lying on the floor. A few feet away she could see what looked like a woman's foot sticking out from behind the couch.

Moving like a shadow, Kahllah slipped through the front door. She knew before she looked behind the couch that whoever the foot belonged to was dead. It appeared to be a woman in her sixties, dressed only in a bathrobe and headscarf. The cause of death was likely the gash in her throat. This could've easily been mistaken for a domestic dispute between mother and son that had gotten out of hand, but the wound was too clean. This was the work of an assassin. Kahllah reached down and touched the woman's cheek, and a smile spread across her masked face when she found that the corpse was warm. The killer was still in the house!

Sounds of struggle came from the kitchen. Crouched low with a blade in hand, she peered inside just in time to see Roth struggling with a figure clad in black. To his credit, Roth put up a good fight, but he was no match for the assassin. There was the whistle of wind, followed by blood spraying the wall just above the stove. It was over for Roth, yet for Kahllah it was only the beginning.

"I was hoping he'd survive long enough to provide me with some information, but it appears . . ." Kahllah's words trailed off when the assassin turned around and she found herself facing . . . herself?! The assassin was wearing a black jumpsuit and combat boots, with a harness strapped to his chest. Aside from being slightly heavier, the figure seemed like an exact replica of Kahllah, even down to the lotus flower in the center of his mask.

Kahllah was so stunned that she only narrowly avoided the blade that the doppelgänger whipped at her. The black-handled knife scraped the side of her mask before embedding itself in the wall just behind her. Moving with impossible speed, the assassin closed the distance between them, clutching a katana. She was ready when the strike came, a violent clash of steel on steel that sent sparks flying. His strength was impressive but wouldn't be enough to save him. She was called the Maiden Sword of Justice for a reason, and he would soon know why.

The two of them circled each other in the small kitchen. She expected him to press again, but he didn't, as if he was taunting her, daring her to attack. So she did. Kahllah's strikes were controlled and strategic, while his were reactionary. He was decent with a sword but no match for her. She struck twice. He managed to block the first, though the second lanced him across the stomach. Had it not been for the protective armor she would've gutted him with her hooked blade. She had him on the defensive now; as he backpedaled, she slammed a boot into his chest, sending him stumbling into the refrigerator, knocking loose several of the cheap magnets that decorated it. A two-handed strike with her hooked sword knocked his katana away, leaving him vulnerable. She put everything behind her next swing, aiming for his head, but he caught it with his hands. The blade was razor-sharp and should've cut clean through his fingers, but it did nothing. Didn't so much as scratch him. She watched in shock as he twisted, bending the steel in on itself.

"My turn," he said in a distorted voice.

Kahllah was fast, faster than most, but the assassin moved with a speed that shouldn't have been possible for a human. She tried to block the first flurry of punches with her forearms, sending shock waves of pain through her limbs. Every time he hit her it was like being struck by a lead pipe. When he slugged her in the gut, the wind was sucked right out of her. She would've collapsed had he not been holding her up by her harness. He slapped her across the face with so much force that it cracked her mask and made something pop in her jaw. This time he allowed her to drop to the ground. When she tried to push to her feet, he kicked her in the stomach and sent her sliding across the kitchen floor.

As Kahllah lay there, almost every inch of her body aching, her mind raced. She knew from the time she had taken her vows and joined the Brotherhood of Blood that dying of old age would never be an option. She often imagined the different ways that she might go out when the reaper finally came to claim what was owed to him, but none of those scenarios ended with her whipped like a dog, waiting to be euthanized and powerless to stop it.

The doppelgänger knelt beside her and ran his hand down her thigh. His touch was cold and hard, even through her clothes. "There is beauty even in broken flowers."

"Be mindful of the thorns." She jerked away. "Get on with it."

"You will die, Kahllah El-Amin, but not today. Just know that the next time you stick your nose where it doesn't belong, I'm going to break your heart instead of your body . . . Until next time." He patted her on her ass before disappearing.

It was a few minutes before Kahllah was able to peel herself from the ground. She wasn't sure what hurt more, her body or her pride. Losing was not something she took well or easily forgot, but the beating had provided her with some insight. There was now no doubt in her mind that the man was part of the Brotherhood; his fighting skills said as much. Whether he had been sent by the Order or was operating independently remained a question. She needed answers, and there was only one place in the city where she knew to get them.

CHAPTER 13

A few hours after his run-in with Kahllah, Detective Wolf found himself longing for nothing more than a cold beer and a hot bath to ease his aching body. Nothing made a man feel his age more than being tossed out of a second-floor window. It could've been worse; he'd seen firsthand what the Lotus was capable of. Near-death experiences aside, he still had a job to do.

If he knew Kahllah like he thought he did, she'd immediately get on the trail of whoever had been involved with Detective Cobb's death, or anyone who could connect her to it. Though Kahllah was an honorable woman, she was also a killer. This meant that nothing could be left to chance or hunches.

In order to find out how Cobb came to his end, she would likely start at the beginning, which was what Wolf planned to do as well. The first place he visited was the precinct that Cobb worked out of. The officers on duty were less than forthcoming in providing him with useful information, because he was a cop who busted other cops. He did, however, stumble across a female clerk who was willing to give him something to go on. She had been romantically involved with the detective until shortly before his death. According to her, Cobb had incurred some gambling debts that he'd been stressed out about. The reason she knew this was because he had borrowed money from her and never paid it back. Her theory was that the people he owed money to were responsible, but Wolf knew that bookies didn't leave calling cards. Still, it was something.

His next stop was Cobb's apartment. He'd gotten the address from the clerk, and figured he could maybe pick up a clue there. Cobb had lived on the fourth floor of a walk-up in East Harlem. Not the most savory neighborhood, but the detective hadn't been a very savory person. Some kids who had been sitting on the front stoop parted like the Red Sea as Wolf passed. They knew trouble when they saw it.

Wolf was slightly winded by the time he reached the fourth floor. He promised himself, as he had repeatedly, that he was going to quit smoking. When he left the stairwell he found the hallway empty, which was a good sign. His visit wasn't authorized, and he could only imagine how it would look if someone caught him picking the lock. Cobb's apartment was at the end of the hall. He planned to get in, find whatever leads he could, and get out. The Lotus already had a head start on him, so he had ground to make up.

Nearly at Cobb's door, Wolf stopped in his tracks when he saw the knob turn and a large man step out. He was wearing dark jeans and a black overcoat. Swinging in his hand was a bowling bag. The guy paused when he saw the detective; he tried to play it cool, but his body language gave him away—he tensed like a child caught with his hand in the cookie jar. Then a warning went off in Wolf's head. One must've gone off in the big man's head too, because as soon as he was close enough, he tried to club Wolf with the bowling bag.

With Wolf thrown off-balance, the guy sprinted right past him. Wolf managed to catch him as he tried to slip into the stairwell, grabbing a handful of the big man's overcoat. The guy promptly spun out of his grip and took off up the stairs. There were only five stories, so there was nowhere for the hulk to go but the roof. Wolf slowed, drawing his gun before stepping through the door that led to the roof. He found the man looking back and forth like a trapped animal. There was nowhere for him to go unless he sprouted wings.

"Look, I'm a cop." Detective Wolf brandished his badge. "I just need to ask you a couple of questions."

"Only words I got for you will be whispered over your corpse," the big man replied, pulling something from the bag he carried. It was too large and shiny to be a bowling ball. It appeared to be a helmet made to look like an elephant's head. The big man slipped it on, rapping his knuckles on the side as if testing the density.

"A little early for Halloween, isn't it?" Wolf chuckled.

"Laugh now, bleed later."

The man charged at Wolf, leading with the crown of his helmet. He made contact at the same moment that Wolf pulled the trigger. The force of the impact knocked the detective off his feet and sent the shot wild. He crashed onto the graveled rooftop, scraping his hands and dropping his gun.

When the elephant raised his massive foot above the detective, Wolf punched him in the nuts. He followed with a combination to the gut that staggered his attacker but didn't drop him; evidently, nothing short of a bullet or Mack Truck could do that. Wolf lunged for his gun, but the big man grabbed him by the ankles before he could reach it. In an incredible show of strength, he swung Wolf around and sent him sailing across the rooftop. Before Wolf could right himself, the brute was back on him. He wrapped his massive hands around Wolf's neck and began squeezing.

As much as Wolf clawed, he couldn't break the grip. Veins bulged in his forehead and his eyes got tight. The man was trying to pop his head like a water balloon. Wolf was seeing blots and knew he'd pass out unless he did something. He ran his hands through the gravel and grasped something jagged. A howl of pain came from the big man when Wolf plunged the metal shard into his thigh.

Now free from the elephant's hold, Wolf scrambled away on his hands and knees. He rested his back against an air duct, sucking in precious air. He'd hoped stabbing the guy would slow him down, but it only seemed to enrage him.

The elephant clutched his wound and glared at Wolf. "First I was going to just beat you to death. Now, you get the horns." He tapped a button on the side of his helmet and two pointed tusks slid from the sides.

"Give it up, man. This is going to end badly for you." Wolf pushed to his feet, his left arm hanging loosely at his side.

The elephant's response was to lower his head and charge once again. Wolf had to time his next move just right. When the brute was within spitting distance, Wolf played his trump card: a length of pipe he had pulled loose from the air duct. He ducked under the tusks and smashed the pipe into the elephant's knee, sending him crashing to the ground. Not taking any chances, the detective brought the pipe down across the back of the man's head so hard that it dented the metal helmet. He was out cold.

"Now," Wolf panted, standing over the unconscious man, "about those questions."

* * *

Two hours after nearly getting his ass kicked for the second time in the span of twenty-four hours, Wolf found himself with more questions than when he started. The elephant man, Benjamin Jordan, was in custody, but he had been less than cooperative. Every question he was asked received one of two responses: "Eat a dick" or "Lawyer." He was as hard as that damn helmet they'd taken off of him.

The helmet itself was another mystery. Wolf had turned it over to the department's tech guys to run some tests on it. So far, they hadn't come up with much. It was made of a metal they couldn't identify, and powered by technology they didn't understand. They'd stopped just short of calling it alien. They would have to send it out to their labs in Albany to learn more, which would take at least a week. Wolf didn't have that kind of time.

When the detective pulled Benjamin Jordan's police file, the situation became even more confusing. The man had been arrested several times, mostly for assault and robbery. Nothing crazy. How the hell did a stickup kid come into possession of something like that helmet? More importantly, how did all this connect to Francis Cobb?

The next page of the file was where things got interesting. It listed known associates of Mr. Jordan. One name in particular stood out to Wolf. He wouldn't have thought much of it, except this was the second time in twenty-four hours that it had come up. This was no coincidence.

CHAPTER 14

The first thing Kahllah noticed when she walked into the restaurant was the heavy smell of curry. She hated curry. As a girl it had been one of her favorite things. She had lived for Sunday dinners, knowing that her mom would make curried goat for the family, a family she no longer had. Now curry served only as a grim reminder of everything that had been taken from her.

She left her mask back in the car and used a short leather jacket to cover the harness holding several blades. Moving through Midtown in the evening, there would be more eyes on her here than in residential Bensonhurst.

The scene from earlier had been playing in her head on repeat since she dragged herself out of the Roth home. It wasn't the first time she had lost a fight, but she hadn't just lost—she got her ass handed to her. The doppelgänger seemed to know her every move before she made it. It was as if he had studied her, but how? He was part of the Brotherhood, that much was obvious, but who was he? Identities were kept closely guarded within the Order, though clearly he knew her. Not only her fighting style, but her name. In the wrong hands, that bit of information could be damning to everyone in her life. This made putting the impostor down even more urgent, but first she needed to find him. Only one person in this city would be able to tell her how.

She arrived at the restaurant around the time most businesses would be preparing for dinner rush, yet the place was relatively empty, save for a few hard-looking souls eating at a table in the back. Behind the bar was a dark-haired man, pretending to restock but really watching her through the mirror. Kahllah sauntered to the bar and slid onto a stool.

The dark-haired man waited a beat before pausing his stocking and turning his attention to her. He was handsome, tanned, with brown eyes and the beginnings of a beard. He gave her a flirtatious smirk before laying a napkin in front of her. "Hello there, beautiful." His voice was rich and deep. "Can I get you a menu or are you just drinking?"

"A beer, please." Kahllah watched as he popped the top off a Corona bottle and set it down in front of her.

"Anything else?" he asked.

"Actually, yes. I'm looking to hire a killer."

"Now that's a good one." He laughed. "Sorry, but all we serve here is cheap alcohol and overseasoned Mediterranean food. Anything else and I'm afraid you've come to the wrong place."

"I was named in the shadow of the mountain," Kahllah recited the Brotherhood's identification code. She now had his attention.

"And my blood has stained its sands," he replied. "I'm—"

"I know exactly who you are. You are Remy St. John, a man who connects those who need to be connected."

"Very good. And who might you be?"

"I'm shocked, Remy. You fraudulently take a contract in my name, yet don't have the decency to recognize karma when it's sitting mere feet away from you." Kahllah shook her head.

"Lotus?" He had never met the assassin in person.

"The one and *only*." She saw Remy's hand inch toward something behind the bar. "Before you reach it, I'll have taken your hand and possibly your head. I want answers, not blood, but I'm fine with both."

"For a member of the Order to harm a broker is forbidden," he reminded her. "A crime punishable by death."

"And so is taking lives in my name. I'm trying to unravel a mystery here, and I think you're the key."

"Me? What do I know? I'm simply a broker. I put people together who need to meet."

"You're also a walking, talking information bank. Nothing goes on within the Brotherhood without you either hearing about it or putting your two cents in it."

"Flattery will get you everywhere, Lotus," Remy joked.

"Who is it that was trying to contract the Black Lotus?"

Remy looked baffled. "I thought you said you're retired."

"I am, which is why I can't understand why lives are being taken in my name. Who is behind these killings?"

"Maybe it was a copycat? You know the Black Lotus has become quite famous over the years. Wouldn't be the first time a zealot has slapped on a mask and pretended to be something they are not."

"This is no zealot. The killer may or may not be a member of the Order, but he was trained by the Brotherhood." Kahllah thought back to how the assassin had bested her. "That much I'm sure of."

"Members of our Order go rogue all the time. Eventually they all meet with the justice deserving of them. I still don't see what this has to do with me."

"Nothing in this city dies at the hands of a Brother unless your seal is on the contract. I'll ask you one last time: who is out there putting blood on my name?"

"I'm afraid you've been misinformed about whatever

my involvement has been in all this. Even if I did issue a contract, which I haven't, we both know that information would be confidential. Now, if we're done here, I'm going to need you to leave. By your own words, you no longer serve our Order."

Her eyes drifted to the mirror, where she noticed that the hard souls were no longer seated at the table in the rear, but loitering close behind her. She doubted they were Brothers, more likely hired muscle. Kahllah had hoped when she came in that she'd be able to reason with Remy. Clearly this would not be the case. "Blood it is then."

There were four of them, dead men who hadn't been put into the ground yet. The first to reach Kahllah was the first to bleed. She spun around on the stool and smashed her beer bottle down over his head. Without missing a beat, she shoved the jagged end into his throat and ripped it open. Seeing his blood spray gave his comrades pause, but not Kahllah. She slid off the stool, drawing two of the blades from the harness under her jacket. The second goon was just clearing his pistol by the time she reached him. If he were smart, he'd have had it out before getting within arm's reach of her. She drove one of her daggers into his wrist, and when he opened his mouth to scream she shoved the second dagger into it. Spinning like a ballerina, she gave the third goon two quick cuts across his face before pushing one of the daggers through his skull. This left the fourth and final attacker, who was armed with a baseball bat.

"I'm not armed!" the man declared, tossing his bat to the ground. He wanted no part in the lethal beauty.

"Your fault, not mine," Kahllah said before opening his throat. When she turned back to the bar, Remy was no longer there. He was making a beeline toward the rear exit. Kahllah flicked a blade at him, and it found a place in the soft flesh of his thigh, sending him to the ground.

"Fucking bitch!" Remy shouted, clutching his bloody leg.

"I've been called worse by better." Kahllah grabbed the back of his shirt and dragged him over to the bar. She took one of the stools and placed it on his chest before sitting on it, making it hard for him to breathe. "I have some questions and you are going to give me the answers."

"I don't know anything!"

"Liar." She pressed down harder on the stool. "Before we get to the fact that you've allowed someone to snatch lives in my name, let's stroll down memory lane a bit. Have you or anyone in your network heard of Tiger Lily resurfacing?"

"Lotus, you haven't been retired that long. Everyone

knows the traitor has been dead for years, undone by her own greed."

"Then who is running around committing crimes using claws that can rip through steel? Is it possible that before Tiger Lily's death she could've entrusted one of her disciples with her claws, or something of the like?"

"Doubtful. She guarded those claws closer than her own children. She would've never gifted them. They likely followed her to the grave. As far as her disciples, the last I heard, most of the bitch's pups were hunted down and executed not long after she was killed. Any who may have been lucky enough to escape the executioner's blade have probably gone underground, and if they know what's best they'll stay there."

"Even Seven-Palms?" The thought had been rolling around in her head since the doppelgänger assassin bent her sword. Elders aside, Seven-Palms was the only one she had seen master such a technique that could bend steel.

"The gimp? His career in the Brotherhood ended years ago. You saw to that. Though I did hear that not long after, he tried to petition the elders to accept him back. They turned him away. A broken man has no place in our ranks. You know this. I know you didn't come all this way to interrogate me about ghosts."

"If this was an interrogation, you'd be bleeding way

more than you are now. Who took the contract in my name?"

"I've already told you that—"

"Wrong answer." She pressed nearly her full weight down on the stool, cutting off his air. She let him gasp for a while before letting up. "Something you want to tell me?"

"Okay, okay . . . I did sign off on the contract."

"Tell me something I don't know. Who paid for it? Was it Chance King?" She remembered how uneasy Magic had been after his exchange with King at Voodoo.

"Who?"

"Don't fuck with me, Remy!"

"I swear, outside of what I've seen on the news, I've never met the man!"

"Then who dropped the bag for the contract?"

Remy didn't answer, so she pressed even harder on the stool.

"John Smith!" Remy blurted out.

"You must think I'm stupid." She twirled one of her daggers between her fingers and angled it at his face.

"That's the name he gave. Of course it wasn't his real name, but I didn't question it because he had a marker."

This gave Kahllah pause. A *marker* was like a referral. It was a totem given to associates of the Brotherhood. It didn't make them members, but granted them access to certain things, such as brokers. It was rare, but in theory a civilian holding a marker could contract a Brotherhood assassin without going through normal channels, so long as they had the money to cover the fee.

"What else can you tell me about the man holding the marker?" Kahllah asked. "What did he look like?"

"I've only met him once. Black guy, real handsome fella. Oh, and he was wearing a gold chain with a pendant shaped like a hat."

"Was it a magician's hat?" Kahllah tried not to let her tone betray the thought that had just crossed her mind.

"It's possible, but I was more focused on taking his money than appraising his jewelry."

"Why me? There are at least a half dozen Brothers in the area who you could've given the contract to. Why risk using my name knowing what would happen if I found out?"

"Money, why else? The guy requested the Black Lotus by name. I knew you were retired, but I ran the ad anyhow, as Priest always did when contracting you. When you didn't respond, I tried to offer him someone else, but he insisted that it had to be you. He even doubled the usual fee to make sure this was done by the Black Lotus."

"And so, your greedy ass went out and found an impostor to do the deed." Kahllah shook her head sadly. "Who did you give the contract to?"

"Lotus, you know the rules. I could be killed for what I've already told you."

"And you will surely die if you don't answer my question."

Remy weighed this for several moments, then said, "Red Death. He's who I got to take the job."

This was a name Kahllah was familiar with. Red Death was a highly skilled killer, but not skilled enough to beat her, and certainly not capable of bending steel with his bare hands. Still, she had to follow up on all possible leads. "Where can I find Red Death?"

"In an unmarked grave somewhere in Westchester. Two days after I gave him the contract, but before he had completed the job, he was taken out. When he missed his scheduled check-in, I sent some of my people to look for him. They found his corpse in his apartment."

"The Brotherhood do him in for falsely taking the contract?"

"If they'd known about it, I'd say so, but they didn't. Besides, he died a most unusual death . . . his neck was broken in two places."

"Garrote?" Kahllah had taken more than her fair share of lives by strangling the victims with wires, iron collars. The method made for a quiet death.

"The finger marks around his neck suggested otherwise. His neck was broken by hands, not a cord."

Same as Roth, she thought. No doubt they had been killed by the same man. The deeper Kahllah dug, the more sense this was all starting to make, though there were still some blanks she needed filled in. "Why would someone kill Red Death to snatch a contract from him that was meant for me in the first place?"

"Your guess is as good as mine," Remy said. "One thing I'm sure of is that whoever this is has a serious hard-on for the Black Lotus."

"You have a knack for pointing out the obvious, Remy. This leads me to my next dilemma. If you can't tell me who this rogue is or where to find him, then I have no use for you." Kahllah raised her dagger.

"Wait! I may not be able to tell you where the rogue is, but I can tell you where he will be." He slowly reached into his pocket, produced a folded printout, and handed it to Kahllah.

She scanned the slip of paper that listed several addresses. One of them she recognized as the Roth home. "What is this?"

"Intel on the target locations that I had gathered for Red Death. Maybe this will help with that itch you're looking to scratch."

"Seems you might not be as useless as I thought."

Kahllah got off the stool and removed it from his chest. She extended her hand to help him up. The moment he took it, she plunged her dagger into his stomach.

"Brothers are forbidden from harming brokers!" Remy moaned, clutching at the blade in his gut.

"I'm retired," she reminded him before ripping his belly open.

It took exactly eight minutes for Remy to finish bleeding out and die. Kahllah knew because she had timed it. She could've killed him swiftly, as she had done his goons, but she wanted him to suffer—he deserved no less. For years Kahllah's adopted father, Priest, had been a broker. Her contracts had always come from him, but when he was no longer able to serve, Remy had been chosen to take his place. When Remy moved into the position, he was bound by honor to place the interests of the Brotherhood above his own. But he had accepted the Black Lotus contract under false pretenses, becoming no better than Tiger Lily. Remy was yet another example of the corruption that was spreading through a once honorable society. More and more young Brothers were placing their finances above their oaths, and it was only a matter of time before the Brotherhood was full of mercenaries motivated by greed instead of principles. The old ways were dying, and Kahllah feared for the Order's future.

She took the time to retrieve whatever surveillance videos she could find from the restaurant, before setting the place ablaze. She didn't want to risk leaving any evidence. She wasn't worried about the police; neither her DNA nor her fingerprints were on file with any of the official law enforcement agencies. The Brotherhood was another story. They would not be happy about one of their brokers being killed and would likely come looking for whoever was behind it, so she cleaned up her tracks.

She looked down at the list of addresses Remy had given her and reflected on what she'd learned from the dead broker. It had been right in front of her all along, but she'd been too busy pretending to be something that she wasn't to see it. None of what was going on had been a coincidence; it was all orchestrated. At least now she had an idea of who was behind it and how to find them. Those who had sought to make a pawn of her were about to feel the full weight of her wrath, including the man who had called himself John Smith. But to the rogue assassin who had used her name in vain, she would gift the most beautiful death of them all.

CHAPTER 15

"I don't like this," Sable said for the fifth time in as many minutes. She was nervous and it showed. She had traded in her tight dress and heels for tan coveralls and work boots. Every so often she would scratch her head through the matted black wig she was wearing. Sable hated synthetic hair because it made her itch.

"Neither do I," Tay agreed. He was dressed the same. They sat in a dark-blue van with the words *McMillian Cleaning Services* stenciled on the sides in white letters.

"Maybe we should wait."

"We been waiting nearly a half hour now. Any longer and we run the risk of missing our window of opportunity."

"I don't like it. First Snake gets himself killed, then Ben goes missing. Maybe it's a sign that we should back off." Sable had found out about Snake, aka Detective Cobb, getting killed on the evening news. They hadn't given much detail, but the fact that he had turned up dead right after the botched robbery was enough to spook her.

"Snake was a fucking degenerate!" Tay said. "That pig had so much beef on the street, I'm surprised it took somebody this long to do him. And Ben, he's always been Magic's little lapdog. He was probably afraid that his master was gonna find out about him running with us."

"As long as we've been running with Ben, you ever known him to be afraid of anything?"

She had a point, though he wouldn't say as much. He needed her on board. "Don't go getting cold feet on me. I need you for this one, baby." He reached for her hand but she withdrew. "Oh, so it's like that? You might be spooked enough to walk away, but I ain't. I need this. If this don't go down, some real unhappy people are gonna want to know why. No telling what I may get to saying to them in the heat of the moment. Angry people tend to let things slip, including secrets."

Sable glared at him. "You can't hold that over my head forever."

"I don't need forever, just one more night. I don't give a fuck what you do once this is over and I get paid. Now get your shit together and let's go to work!"

They had come to a facility that rented out multiple office suites inside. It was after-hours, so the place was quiet. A lone security guard sat behind a small desk reading a magazine. He looked up briefly when Tay and Sable walked in wearing their fake cleaning gear, pushing a bin that held their supplies. With a simpleton's grin, Tay flashed the dummy badge clipped onto his coveralls. The guard gave it a hard glance before waving them past.

When they were safely inside the elevator, Sable breathed a sigh of relief. Her stomach had been doing flip-flops since they'd left the van. She wished she'd taken a bump before setting out on this fool's errand, but cocaine would've likely made her nerves worse. She just needed to survive the night and she was done with Tay and his bullshit. At this point she didn't care who learned about her snitching.

"Look alive." Tay snapped her out of her thoughts. He had just pulled his wizard's mask and wand out of the bin and was gearing up. "You ready for this?"

"Does it matter?"

He tossed Sable her claws and fox mask. "Look, we're only two instead of four, but the plan is the same: I'll take the guards and you grab the hard drive. Any of these lab geeks try and play hero, give them the business end of them claws." He powered on his wand. "Now let's go get paid."

Their destination was the top floor of the building. It was said to be closed for renovations, but that was an excuse to keep anyone from going up and poking around. When the elevator doors opened, they immediately smelled burning chemicals. The foul scent fell somewhere between rotten eggs and broccoli that had been left out overnight. Tay walked out, wand charged and ready for trouble. He had expected to encounter a guard posted by the elevator, but as luck would have it, no one was there.

From the end of the hall they could hear the low hum of machines at work. Tay moved with stealth toward the noise with Sable watching his back. They approached a smoked-glass door with a prop-up sign marked *DO NOT ENTER*. The smell was strongest there. He glanced over his shoulder at Sable. He could tell she was still nervous, but was sure once it popped off she would stand tall as she always did.

"Where are the guards?" she whispered. If what they were out to steal was as valuable as Tay had claimed, it struck her as odd that it wouldn't be better protected.

"No clue, but whatever rock they're hiding under is the one they'll die under if they give us grief. Just keep your head on swivel. You ready?" In response, Sable extended her claws. "That's my girl."

Tay went through the door first. If they thought the stench was powerful in the hallway, inside the office suite it was overwhelming. The room was dark, save for the flickering of the emergency lights that appeared every few feet along the walls. Set up on several tables were glass beakers atop small burners. One of the heated beakers was bubbling over, spilling a pale-blue liquid onto the table. According to the backer, this was an operation of major importance, but to Tay it looked like a neglected high school science lab.

"Something isn't right." Sable's foot had just landed in something sticky that she couldn't identify.

There was a stir of motion to her left, causing her to spin. A figure shambled through the shadows, something long and thick dangling from its hand. Sable's first thought was that it was a club or sawed-off shotgun, but when the person got close enough, she saw it was neither. In fact, it wasn't a weapon at all but an arm—a man's arm. Someone had cut his left arm off at the elbow, and he was carrying the bloody limb in his right hand.

"What the fuck?" Sable gasped. Just then the overhead lights came to life, temporarily blinding her. When her eyes adjusted, she saw her surroundings and wished she hadn't.

The mystery of where everyone had gone was solved. They were dead. Corpses lined the floor of the spacious room. They had all been butchered, some missing limbs, others without heads. This was no lab. It was a slaughterhouse.

"Beloved," a strange, mechanical voice seemed to come from everywhere at once, "never avenge yourself, but leave it to the wrath of God; for it is written, *Vengeance is mine, I will repay*, says the Lord." Kahllah emerged from the shadows in the corner. She was armed with a kyoketsu-shoge, a short blade attached to a length of chain. She had been expecting the rogue, but it seemed he'd sent his accomplices. "I see the devil has employed helpers."

"Who the fuck are you supposed to be?" Tay asked, looking at the strange getup consisting of a mask and harness. Before taking on the job, he had been assured that the only resistance they might encounter would be a few hired guns, but the person standing before him was clearly more than that.

"I am the Maiden Sword . . . the purifier . . . I am that which will usher in the end of days." She swung the chain over her head twice before whipping it at Tay. The strike would've been the end of him, had one of Sable's iron claws not deflected it. Seeing the claws, Kahllah had to swallow a rush of anxiety, recalling the scarring of her young flesh. She shook the feeling off. This fox was not Tiger Lily, and Kahllah was no longer a naive, approval-seeking girl. She was the Black Lotus . . . She was death!

Sable absorbed the weight of the assassin's next blow with her gauntlet, and felt her wrist snap inside of it. A sharp elbow to her jaw knocked away the fox mask, exposing her face. It was then that the assassin paused.

"You!" Kahllah hissed. It was the same girl she had seen at Voodoo. If this was Sable, the man had to be Tay. This confirmed her suspicion that it was all a setup.

Sable used Kahllah's brief moment of indecision to make her next move. She lashed out wildly, and the assassin stumbled backward, seemingly flustered. Sable went in for the kill, but the assassin flung the chain around her ankles, throwing her off-balance. In the same motion, the bladed end of Kahllah's weapon came whipping across her torso.

Sable thanked her stars that it hadn't connected, but then she saw the blood. She tore away the front of her coveralls and stared, in wide-eyed horror, as her intestines came spilling out. "Tay," her voice trembled. She fell.

"Nooooo!" Tay howled.

Kahllah looked down at the unconscious girl. When she spoke to Tay, her voice was almost apologetic. "They say that at the moment of death, all the mistakes we've made in life flash before our eyes. Hers, and yours, was not knowing how to leave well enough alone. And now you'll die for it."

"Fuck you!" Tay roared, and slammed his wand on the floor.

Kahllah was unprepared for the powerful shock

wave that followed. She felt like someone had knocked the wind out of her, and she crashed through one of the tables that held beakers. Glasses shattered, and when the blue liquid touched the open flame of a burner, it ignited. A series of small explosions went off around the room, and it wasn't long before the air was filled with rancid chemical smoke.

"I'm going to kill you!" Tay coughed, sweeping his wand back and forth. Smoke invaded his eyes and nose and obscured everything. The sound of glass crunching under boots caused him to turn. The assassin was coming through the smoke, spinning the bladed chain like a helicopter. Tay tried to use his wand again, but this time Kahllah was ready; the blade bisected the wand just before it reached the ground. There was a nasty surge of whatever powered the weapon, and Tay dropped it.

Kahllah stalked toward him. "And so, the wolf becomes the sheep. You should've left while you could, but you didn't, and now here we are."

"Look, whatever Magic's paying, I'll double it," Tay offered. This whole setup stank of Magic. Besides himself and his backer, the only person who knew in advance the location of the lab they'd planned to hit was the one person conveniently absent. Ben had crossed them. That had to be it. If Tay survived this, he would settle up with both of his former partners.

"Magic will have his day, but this dance is yours," Kahllah said. "Will you repent before I send you to join your friend at the feet of our Lord and Savior?"

As if on cue, a guttural scream erupted behind her. It happened so fast that Kahllah didn't have a chance to stop it. Sable came leaping through the fire like a mad-woman, eyes wild. Her iron claws sliced a part of Kahl-lah's side unprotected by armor. Ignoring the explosive pain, Kahllah whipped her weapon out and lassoed the girl's neck.

Tears welled in Sable's eyes as she knew the end was at hand. With her last breath, she asked a favor of her killer: "Tell Magic . . . I never stopped loving him."

Kahllah nodded before yanking the chain. Sable's head made a faint snapping sound as it came off her shoulders, rolling to a stop at Kahllah's feet. Her eyes stared up at the assassin accusingly. Even in death the girl's face was just as beautiful as the first time Kahllah had seen her. What could her life have been, had she not fallen in with the enemies of the Lotus? She said a quick prayer for the misguided girl before turning back to Tay. Unfortunately, there was no sign of him. While his lover was being killed, he'd slipped out a back door. It didn't matter. She had his scent; he could crawl into a hole and still not find refuge from her blades.

As Kahllah was making her way from the burning

structure, a vibrating sensation startled her. It was her cell phone, tucked into one of the pockets of her harness. She was hardly up for conversation, especially with the man whose name flashed across the screen. She'd almost forgotten about Dominic and the way she'd left things. At the last second, she decided she owed him an answer. "Dom, this isn't really a good time," she said while rushing down the back stairs.

"Guess again," an unfamiliar voice replied.

Kahllah stopped in her tracks. "Who is this? Where's Dominic?"

"Dom can't come to the phone right now."

"If you've hurt him—"

"Your boyfriend is good, but I can't say for how long. I told you that the next time you involved yourself in my business I was going to break your heart instead of your body. You've broken your vow to love none above the Order, Lotus. I'm surprised at you."

"What do you want?"

"What I've always wanted . . . *you*. If you want to save your boyfriend, meet me at the place where it all ends. Humble yourself before your betters and he may just survive the night. Don't keep me waiting too long, little *bruja*." He hung up.

The man didn't need to tell her where he was. *Where it all ends* was something said among the Brotherhood. It referenced a predetermined spot where a sworn member would execute their last kill, before ending their service to the Order. There was only one place all this could end for Kahllah.

CHAPTER 16

Picking a lock on his knees in an alley reminded Detective Wolf of his days before the police force. Growing up, he had been good at two things: stealing and boxing. The former brought him the most joy. Unlike most kids, who stole out of necessity, Wolf stole to piss his parents off. His dad was a blues singer, and ran the household with an iron fist. He kept his kids on the straight and narrow, despite having a cocaine addiction, and when they strayed they got the business end of his belt. Wolf used to resent his dad for being so hard on him, but when he got older he understood that his father was just preparing him to go out into a cold and unforgiving world.

Wolf was sure he could've gotten a search warrant for the place, but that would have taken time, a luxury he didn't have. Things were unfolding faster than he had expected. Since securing his prisoner, he had been tuning in to the police scanner as all hell seemed to be breaking loose around the city. A reported grease fire at a restaurant, an explosion on an unoccupied floor of an office building—the city was jumping. To the department the events seemed random, but Wolf suspected otherwise.

It was his fault, really. Kahllah was carving a path of destruction in the name of her honor, and he had allowed her the freedom to do it. A sensible man would've taken her in and sorted it all out later, but Wolf had never been sensible. Besides, he wasn't okay with arresting people he didn't believe were guilty. Kahllah was no saint, but Wolf knew what she was about. Though there might've been plenty of blood on her hands, it was unlikely that any of it was Cobb's. The only way to put an end to this would be to either catch the real perp, or put down someone he had come to almost consider a friend. There was no way she would come quietly. This was what had him breaking into a nightclub like a common thief.

Originally, he had planned on just walking in the front door and causing a scene, as he was known to do, but the club wasn't open tonight. That wouldn't stop him from finding what he sought, which was something that tied Magic to what was going on. When he'd first been put on Magic's scent, Wolf worried that he was chasing his own tail with the lead, but that changed when he reached out to some of his street contacts to see what he could learn about the character. Much to his surprise, Magic was heavier in the game than he thought, or at least he had been. According to his sources, Magic used to run with a crew that had been responsible for some high-stakes robberies over the years. At their height, they were considered the best at what they did. Their signature was high-tech weapons that no one else on the streets had access to. This would explain Ben's helmet. He tried to probe deeper to see if he could get a line on who was supplying the weapons, but no one would talk. It was a question he would have to ask Magic once he found him. Hopefully his little B-and-E would provide him with some clue as to how.

The door he entered through put him in a storage room. Cases of crates bearing different liquor stamps sat all over; judging from the number, Voodoo must host a lot of thirsty patrons night in and night out. There was enough liquor to water all of Times Square on New Year's Eve. Wolf drew his gun before moving deeper. The place appeared to be empty, but he wasn't taking any chances. If the helmet Ben had attacked him with was any indication of what types of weapons these guys were carrying, there was no telling what Magic would be armed with.

As he was moving through the darkened room, he accidentally knocked over one of the liquor crates. He tensed, waiting for the loud crash that would surely announce his presence, but there was nothing. Curious, he bent down and picked the crate up. It was too light to hold bottles, though it wasn't empty. With a knife he pried open its top. Wolf was surprised when he peered inside and, instead of finding champagne as was stamped on the crate, he found what looked like cocaine. There were several neatly wrapped parcels inside. He suspected the other boxes carried the same.

Legitimate businessman my ass, Wolf chuckled to himself. He'd come looking for a way to connect Magic to Cobb's murder, and had instead stumbled upon what would likely be a career-making drug bust.

"Find what you were looking for, Detective?" a voice came from behind Wolf. He turned and found a man aiming a gun at him.

The face was familiar to Wolf. He had seen him before, more than once. "You!" the detective blurted out, but his voice was muted by the sound of the gun going off. Wolf felt a searing burn when the bullet took him off his feet. He had heard stories from some of his comrades about what it felt like to be shot, and though each story differed, the one thing they had in common was the burning. It was as if Wolf's body had been set on fire. The pain only lasted a few seconds but it felt like forever, and then came the numbness. Euphoria settled over him. It was so relaxing, he would perhaps sleep for a week if he closed his eyes. After all the running around over the last couple days, sleep sounded good. He was tired . . . oh so tired. As he drifted off into peaceful oblivion, his last thoughts were that Kahllah had been telling the truth about being innocent and he would never have a chance to apologize for doubting her.

Kahllah felt an eerie cold settle in her bones as she stood at the entrance of Voodoo. The last time she had visited, it had been alive with activity, but tonight it was dark and seemed more ominous. Without question, she was walking into a trap, but what choice did she have? Somewhere inside the man she cared deeply about was in danger, and it was her fault. In her mind she could hear her father's warning to her the day she received her mask: *The vows you have taken are very much like those a bride takes on her wedding day. Promise to love, honor, and obey this sacred Order above all others for the rest of your days. You are a weapon now, nothing more. The minute you allow yourself to forget that, the Brotherhood will remind you.*

At the time she didn't understand, but now, as she stood before the nightclub, it all made sense. Every time she allowed someone to get close to her, the Brotherhood took them away. She couldn't let that happen to Dominic. Once she freed him from his captors, she would free him from her. He hadn't broken his vows, she had.

Kahllah wasn't surprised to find the front doors unlocked. They were expecting her. As she walked down the dark hall toward the main area, she remained vigilant in the event that there were more minions involved than the ones she'd faced at the lab. An honorable member of the Brotherhood would've faced her straight up, but her enemy had already proved himself dishonorable, just like the one who had spawned him.

The main area was better lit than the hall, but only slightly. The bar, as well as the dance floor, were shrouded in darkness. Over the VIP area shone a single light, above the table she and Audrey had been seated at the other day. This was where she found Dominic. He was sitting in a chair with his hands shackled behind him. A blindfold covered his eyes, and a length of cloth, secured with tape, gagged him. She picked her way through the room, kyoketsu-shoge in hand, poised to strike out at an instant. Closer, she got a better look: he was a little roughed up, and his shirt was torn, but he seemed otherwise unharmed. When she removed his blindfold, Dominic blinked against the light. The sight of her mask spooked him, and he recoiled in fear. She knelt before him. "Dominic, relax. It's me." She took off her mask. "I'm going to get you out of here," she said, removing his gag.

"Kahllah?" His reaction was one of both surprise and relief. "What are you doing here? And what are you wearing?"

"Dom, I'm sorry that you got caught up in this, and I promise to answer all your questions, but first let me get you somewhere safe."

"You mean to tell me there's a party going on in my spot and I wasn't invited?" Magic said as he walked in. He had a sawed-off shotgun braced against his hip and pointed at Kahllah. But when he recognized her, a look of shock crossed his face. "What are *you* doing here?"

"You brought me." She rose to her feet, eyes burning with anger. Her kyoketsu hung at her side. "You requested an audience with the Black Lotus, and so you have it, Magic. Or would you prefer if I called you John Smith?"

"John *who*? I got a notification that the silent alarm went off, and thought somebody was robbing me. I was expecting a burglar, not a crazed journalist in her pajamas. I don't know what's going on, but you'd better tell me something or I'm going to let this pump sort it out." Magic pulled the slide.

Kahllah studied his eyes for signs of deception, but found none. This wasn't making sense. All signs pointed to him being John Smith, but what if she had been wrong? What if this was yet another strange twist in what was proving to be her most bizarre mission to date?

Magic, seeming to sense that there was something more, looked like he was about to lower his shotgun, until he spotted Dominic tied to the chair. "What the—"

was as far as he got before the top of his head exploded.

Tay stood over Magic's corpse holding a smoking gun. "I knew setting off that alarm would draw you out into the open." His face and coveralls were still stained with Sable's blood. There was a maddened lilt to his voice when he spoke, like a man close to the edge. "You always did love your dreams more than you loved us. I tried to tell Sable you weren't about *shit*." He spat on the body before firing two more bullets into it. "She wanted you to have those, by the way."

"And what prompts a dog to turn on its master?" Kahllah wondered out loud.

"This coming from the bitch he hired to kill his own people?" Tay shot back. "Magic thought he could play me for a fool, and look what it got him."

"I was no more in the service of Magic than he was John Smith." Kahllah chuckled as she stared down at the corpse. Not because she found the situation funny, but because she had allowed herself to be so easily manipulated. "It would appear that we've both been played for fools by someone tonight, and I doubt it was Magic."

"Bullshit!" Tay spat. "You're lying trying to save your ass. I know it was Magic who put you on us."

"No, I'm afraid she's telling the truth," said a voice from the dark bar area. He had been sitting so still that one could've easily mistaken him for a statue or some other inanimate object. It was the man who had engineered it all, the doppelgänger. "The Black Lotus was indeed dispatched to kill your team, but it was I who set it in motion, not Magic. You killing him was an unexpected twist."

"What, did Party City have a sale on Halloween costumes?" Tay looked from the impostor to Kahllah and back. "The fuck are you?"

"His name is Seven-Palms," Kahllah said.

"Very good, Lotus." The impostor nodded at her. "Though I haven't gone by that name in years, thanks to you. These days I am called Golden Arm." He removed one of his black gloves and revealed a mechanical hand the color of gold. "Beautiful, isn't it? This new arm was Tiger Lily's last gift to me before the Brotherhood betrayed her."

Kahllah laughed. "You are as delusional now as you were when you stepped into the circle thinking you could beat me. It was Tiger Lily who betrayed us when she placed her finances above her vows."

"Is that the lie the Order is spewing to cover what they did?" Golden Arm shook his head. "Tiger Lily was always loyal to the Order. The things she did were never about money; they were about progress. The Brotherhood is dying because they are stuck in their antiquated ways. Tiger Lily was seeking to usher in a new day, and for that they wanted her killed. But for as long as there is breath in my body, her legacy will live on."

"Then let's make this quick." Kahllah started swaying her bladed chain. The two killers squared off, but before they could engage, the sound of a gunshot filled the room.

Tay stood there holding his smoking pistol in the air. "I hate to break up this little reunion of yours, but have the two of you forgotten that there's a man standing here with a gun?"

"Ah, yes, how could I forget you, Tay?" Golden Arm said. "You were my wild card in all this. He who is willing to betray his own for the promise of riches. I have to admit, I didn't expect you to outlive the others. I guess you've proven yourself the most resourceful. That's something I didn't see coming when we first met."

"Homey, I don't know you from a can of paint," Tay responded.

"Oh, right. You probably don't recognize me wearing this." Golden Arm removed his mask. This was the first time Kahllah had ever seen his face. He was handsome, with olive skin and black hair that was neatly cropped at his ears.

"You?" Tay couldn't hide his shock. It was the man who had been supplying his crew with their weapons.

"Yes, your beloved benefactor," Golden Arm confirmed.

"This doesn't make sense. We were your partners. You gave us the toys and in return we put a lot of money in your pocket. Why fuck it all up by trying to have us killed?"

"Oh, did you think you were special?" Golden Arm smiled. "Magic already had a preexisting arrangement with us for the weapons, but he no longer wanted to play the game. I could've picked any number of street rats to arm and send off on a fool's errand, but taking the time to train and properly motivate them would've caused me to miss my window of opportunity. Your group already knew the weapons, and you, Tay, were all too eager to prove to Magic that you were a better leader. So you made the perfect candidate. You were so thirsty to hold the reins of power that you never stopped to wonder why it was so easy for an underqualified thug like you to usurp Magic's connect." He laughed. "Did you really think you could ever walk a mile in Magic's shoes? For all Magic's faults, he was an honorable man and a good leader. He earned my respect. *You* are nothing."

Tay felt like shit on a stick. All this time he had prided himself on the fact that he'd earned his position at the head of the table, that the benefactor dealt with him from a place of respect. The whole time, he had been nothing more than a pawn. The worst part was that Sable had gotten killed because of it. "Muthafucka!"

He raised his gun. Before he could fire, however, Golden Arm shot him once in the chest, taking him off his feet.

Golden Arm stood over Tay holding a sleek pistol, the same one he had used to kill Detective Cobb. "Don't feel bad, Tay. You can't win a chess game without sacrificing a few pawns. Now, go and be with your lover." He shot Tay in the head, ending him. With that out of the way, he turned back to the Black Lotus. "You and I have some unfinished business." His mechanical hand rotated. "You took something from me, and I intend to take *everything* from you." His eyes landed on Dominic, who looked about ready to wet himself.

"Don't." Kahllah moved in front of him protectively.

"No need to fret, Lotus. You won't have to watch your lover die. On my honor, I'll kill him last."

"You speak of honor, yet you bring a gun to a duel. If this is to be the end, then let us observe the rules of combat."

"Very well." Golden Arm tossed the gun to the ground. "Let's finish this."

Kahllah whirled her kyoketsu over her head, then hurled the bladed end, narrowly missing Golden Arm's face. He countered with a spinning kick to her side that knocked the wind out of her. Before she could recover, he was on her again. He tried to punch through the back of her head, but she moved at the last moment. When his fist hit the floor, the tiles cracked. She danced out of his reach and tried to get her second wind.

"Running will only delay the inevitable, Lotus." Golden Arm charged toward her.

Kahllah managed to avoid his mechanical hand, but took an elbow to the jaw. She struck back with the tip of her blade to his stomach; it failed to even pierce his skin. Her third strike hit his vulnerable spot from the first time they met, the crook of his arm, but it had no effect. He responded by slamming his palm into her chest and sending her skidding across the floor. Kahllah rolled to a stop near where Tay's corpse lay.

"I am a living weapon." He grabbed her neck and lifted her. She could feel his metal fingers crushing her windpipe. "Did our first encounter not teach you that I cannot be defeated by a blade?"

"I know," she croaked.

Golden Arm felt something press into his stomach and looked down. In Kahllah's hand was Tay's gun. A thunderous boom sounded when she pulled the trigger. Golden Arm released her and staggered backward. "The rules of combat," he rasped.

"Fuck the rules and fuck you!" Kahllah pulled the trigger again and again, lighting him up. Golden Arm's body did a sick dance, spinning this way and that, until the last shot sent him crashing through a window and out into the street. It was finally done.

When Kahllah's adrenaline stopped pumping, she felt as if her legs were rubber. She had to brace herself against a table to keep from falling. Golden Arm had done more damage than she thought and had likely caused some internal bleeding. She needed a hospital, but first she had to get Dominic out of here. The police would likely arrive soon with questions she wasn't prepared to answer.

"Are you okay?" Kahllah asked, limping over to Dominic.

"I should be asking you. Kahllah, what is all this?"

"This is why we can never be," she sighed. "Look, I promise to explain all of this once I get you out of here." She cut his legs free and then leaned over him to release his chained wrists. At that moment Kahllah paused. Something glinted beneath his torn shirt. It was a necklace of simple gold with a pendant shaped like a magician's hat. A warning went off in her head, but not before pain exploded in her back. Kahllah threw herself backward and landed on her broken ribs. The pain that shot through her side was so intense she almost blacked out. She watched in shock as Dominic got up from the chair, holding the bloody knife that he had been hiding the whole time.

"You like it?" He brandished the necklace. "I got it a few years back from my cousin Magic. That's before we fell out. He has one just like it . . . well, *had*." Dominic motioned toward Magic's corpse.

"I don't understand," Kahllah wheezed. It felt like the knife had punctured her lung, and she found it hard to breathe. Her mind raced, trying to figure out why this man she cared about had just stabbed her.

"Then let me lay down some history," Dominic began. "Before I was straitlaced Dominic, I was Red, a wannabe criminal who had gotten in over his head. I had blown my shot at college and burned the only dude who ever looked out for me and was living from pillar to post. I had hit my bottom, as they call it. That's when Tiger Lily and Golden Arm found me. I was too old to be initiated into the Brotherhood but not totally useless. Under Tiger Lily I got an education that I couldn't have gotten in ten years of college. She taught me about strength, honor, and, more importantly, loyalty. She cleaned me up and paid for me to go back to school. The only thing she ever asked in return was that I remain loyal. That was more than a fair exchange."

"So it was Tiger Lily who sent you after me?" Kahllah asked.

"Hardly," he chortled. "You weren't even a blip on the radar to my mistress. That was Golden Arm. He hated you for what you had done to him, and that hate was only intensified when we discovered that it was you who had been chosen to take her seat on the Council. He blamed you for taking everything from him that he ever cared about. Honestly, he was quite obsessed with you. I couldn't understand it, so I had to see what you were made of for myself. You were retired, so I came up with a plan to draw you out, which was no easy task."

"So you took on the Jerome Yates case just to get close to me?"

"No, that was dumb luck. I really was advocating to get the man released. I know how it feels to be the underdog. When I found out that you were also involved, I took it as the universe giving me a sign. Through Yates I was able to get to know Kahllah El-Amin, though I was more interested in the Black Lotus. Throwing money at you wasn't working, so I had to take a different approach. I had to use the one thing that I knew you held in higher regard than cash."

"My honor."

"Correct. In my time studying you, I came to understand that your reputation was the one thing you would protect at all costs."

"You kill a cop and try and pin it on me to force my hand. I get that part, but why the wild goose chase with the others?" Her breathing was becoming more labored and her vision was starting to blur, but she couldn't pass out. Not until she heard it all.

Dominic shrugged. "It's like I said: I had to see the legendary Black Lotus in action with my own eyes, and let me tell you, you did not disappoint. Watching you kill is like poetry. I can't help but imagine what could've been if you and I had worked together to reshape the Brotherhood. Our children's children could've ruled the Order for generations."

"You sound like just as much of a nut as Tiger Lily and Golden Arm."

"Yes, Golden Arm was a bit eccentric, but Lily was a visionary. She saw what could be, as do I. The old ways of the Order must be purged so that we can usher in a new era."

"Did you ever really care about me?" Kahllah asked.

Dominic weighed the question. "Yes. Maybe not at first, but as I got to know you, I grew to not only care about you but respect you as well. It's easy for me to see why Tiger Lily wants you out of the way. You represent a threat to what she's trying to build."

"She lives then?"

"At this point it's an irrelevant question. The time for talking has passed. Now it ends."

"I couldn't agree more. Did you get all that?"

"Sure did." Detective Wolf appeared behind Dominic. He was covered in blood, and looked as if he could barely keep his feet under him, but the shotgun he had retrieved from Magic's corpse was very steady, and aimed at Dominic.

"But how?" Dominic said. "I shot you!"

"Yes, you did, but this old dog ain't so easy to kill." Wolf collapsed in a chair. Sweat covered his face, and blood dripped onto the floor from the wound in his gut.

"Well played, Lotus." Dominic laughed. "So, what now? I'm supposed to go quietly off to prison? I think we all know that isn't going to happen."

"Who said anything about prison? Cop killers don't go to jail, they go to hell," Wolf said before pulling the trigger and bringing Dominic's game to an end.

EPILOGUE

Kahllah would spend the next few days in the hospital recovering from her wounds. She had two broken ribs, a punctured lung, and a hairline fracture to her jaw. Had the ambulance not arrived when it did, she likely would have died at Voodoo.

Of course, the police had a million questions that needed answers. Thanks to Detective Wolf she at least had some semblance of an alibi. According to the report Wolf filed, Cobb had been working undercover on a drug case. He had gotten in deep with a crew that was moving heavy weight. When the guys he was working with found out he was a cop, they killed him. It was a tip from Ms. El-Amin that led Wolf to Voodoo. She was also investigating the cartel for an exposé that she planned on writing. This is how she and her boyfriend, a respected lawyer, ended up being taken hostage. Wolf staged a one-man rescue mission, which resulted in three of the cartel members getting gunned down, him taking a bullet, and the attorney getting killed. Kahllah had been at Voodoo interviewing the owner, and had the files to prove it.

This would explain how she was tied into it, but the rest of the story was shaky at best. Internal affairs would probably be crawling up Wolf's ass for months about it. But between all the cocaine that had been found at Voodoo and Lieutenant Tasha Grady claiming that she'd signed off on Cobb's deep-cover operation, there wasn't much anyone could do about it. Wolf made headlines for the drug bust and catching the cop killer, while *Real Talk* got the exclusive on both.

It was a win for everybody—so why did Kahllah still feel like a loser?

She was sitting in her hospital bed, reading the article that Audrey had written on everything that had happened. She had to admit, her girl was shaping up to be one hell of a writer. She was proud of her, but having trouble enjoying the moment. Her body was broken, though it wasn't the first time and she knew her physical wounds would heal. Her heart was a different story. She couldn't believe she'd been so wrong about Dominic. Love had made her a fool, and it had almost come at the cost of her life. It was just as her father had warned: *Promise to love, honor, and obey this sacred Order above all others for the rest of your days. You are a weapon now, nothing more. The minute you allow yourself to forget that, the Brotherhood will remind you.* He had been right. A part of her hated him for that, but she would take the lesson to heart. Love truly had no place in her life.

Something else that had been weighing on her was learning that the traitor Tiger Lily hadn't been killed as rumored. If she was still alive—out there somewhere, scheming—what would it mean for the Brotherhood? More importantly, what would it mean for her? Kahllah had killed two of Tiger Lily's disciples and ruined whatever plans she had to usurp the Order. Dominic and Golden Arm were the first to come at her, but there would no doubt be others. She was a threat to Tiger Lily's plans; Dominic had already told her as much.

"Knock knock." Wolf appeared in the doorway. He was wearing a hospital gown, with an IV bag hooked to his wheelchair and an attractive nurse pushing him. His hair was fuzzy, needing to be rebraided, but aside from that and a few scratches, he looked good. "Can I come in?"

"Sure." Kahllah waved him in.

Wolf allowed the nurse to push him to her bedside before whispering something to her. She nodded, and then left them alone to talk. "How are you feeling?"

"Like I've been stabbed and had the shit kicked out of me." She smiled; Wolf didn't.

"You know, you had me kind of shook for a minute. You lost a lot of blood, and for a while they weren't so sure you'd pull through."

"I guess this old dog ain't so easy to kill either. How are you?"

Wolf shrugged. "Lost some blood, and I'll be shitting in a bag for a while because of the gutshot, but I'm alive, so I guess I got no complaints. Even if I did complain, who would listen?"

"I'd listen," Kahllah said. "Wolf, I want to thank you for what you did for me back there. If you hadn't come along, no telling if I'd have made it out or not. You saved my ass."

"Like you've saved mine how many times? I'd say we're square. I should've never doubted you in the first place. I'm sorry for that."

"I can't say I blame you. I don't know if I'd have believed me either if the roles were reversed. That was one hell of a story you spun to make this all sound believable. How'd you get it to fly, and not have to come clean about the Brotherhood and the weapons?"

"To be honest, I didn't. That was a friend of mine in the department. After the last time one of you went off the rails, they put certain protocols in place." Wolf thought about what Grady had told him. "No clue what she meant, but I trust that Tasha. She's got it under control."

"The stuff you said about Magic being a high-ranking member of the cartel . . . was it true, or just fluff for our alibi?"

"Afraid that part was true. He may not have been

tied to the killings, but he was sitting on enough cocaine to make a serious move. Some of my guys on the street cosigned it too. Magic was a player. Sorry, I know you were rooting for the kid to win."

"Guess I'm not as good a judge of character as I thought. And what about the bodies from inside the club?" Kahllah was wondering if the Brotherhood had come to claim what belonged to them.

"All three of them are tucked in the city morgue."

"Don't you mean four?"

"No, there was Magic, his buddy in the coveralls, and your lawyer friend. That was it."

Kahllah could feel the color drain from her face. She had shot Golden Arm at least four times and knocked him out of a window. There was no way he could still be alive, could he? He had said he was a living weapon. If he was still out there, he would return for another shot at her.

If the day came, she would be ready and waiting.

"Everything okay?" Wolf asked, noticing the change in her expression.

She smiled. "Sure, everything is just fine."

"Detective, if you're done here, it's time for your sponge bath." The nurse had returned.

"Well, that's my cue." Wolf patted Kahllah's leg. The nurse made to wheel him out, but he stopped her short. There was one last question he needed answered. "What was with the guy we found in the trunk of that Civic you were driving?"

Kahllah clamped her hand over her mouth. She had totally forgotten about the young man whom she had held captive for nearly ten hours. "Long story. Is he okay?"

"Shaken and a little confused, but otherwise fine. Want to tell me what that was about?"

"It's a story we'll keep for another time."

"I'll hold you to that. Well, I guess I'll see you on the streets, huh, kid?"

"No, I don't think you will, Detective."

Wolf understood what she meant. It would seem his favorite assassin was finally done. "Time will tell, Kahllah. Time will tell." He winked, then motioned for the nurse to continue.

As Wolf was being wheeled out, another man was walking in. They exchanged curious glances, but neither spoke. The sight of the man immediately darkened Kahllah's mood. He was tall with a shaved head and a patch over his left eye. Instead of his usual cassock, he was dressed in black slacks and a gray blazer with a white shirt. In his hand was a small bouquet.

"What do *you* want?" Kahllah said.

"Is that any way to greet a concerned parent?" Priest took the empty chair at her bedside.

"Concerned? I haven't seen you in months, and you pop up out of the blue talking about concern?"

"You're right. I should have been here. Had I, this may not have happened. I promise you, those responsible will be made to pay for what they've done to you."

"You're a little late for that." Kahllah thought of the trail of corpses she had left spread out across the city.

"Am I?" Priest folded his hands on his lap.

Kahllah wasn't sure what he was implying, but with him she knew it was nothing good. "Listen, I'm tired. State your business and leave so I can get some rest."

"Very well." Priest leaned forward and spoke in a hushed tone: "I know you've been through a lot. Take whatever time you need to heal, but when you're well enough, I have someone who requires the services of the Black Lotus."

Kahllah shook her head. "The fucking nerve of you! I almost died thanks to you leaving your responsibilities in the hands of a hack, and now you stroll in and have the nerve to ask me to take another contract?"

"This isn't about money, it's about blood," Priest explained. There was fire in his eyes. "I would not bring this to you had I any other choice, but I don't."

This got Kahllah's attention. In all the time she had known Priest, she couldn't recall ever seeing him this shaken up. She wanted to turn him away but couldn't. "What's happened?"

"The bastard child of Harlem has finally gotten in over his head, and I fear it will take our combined efforts to get him out of it. Please, help me save my son."